Joe

Love Suga

Easter 2008

HEINEMANN
NEW WINDMILLS

SKULKER WHEAT

In this book you'll meet some of the local characters who lived in a village in the Midlands over thirty years ago.

There's old George Cummings, who knows all the ways of farming and life in the country. And old Gaffer, the teacher they loved to tease. And the Football Pools Winner – how does he cope with being rich?

You'll read about the adventures of Jud Price, Woolly Lamb and their friends, too. Like the miracle at the auction. Skulker Wheat's metal catapult. And the day they slaughtered Chunny's pig.

SKULKER WHEAT
and other stories

John Griffin

HEINEMANN EDUCATIONAL BOOKS
LONDON

Heinemann Educational Books Ltd
Halley Court, Jordan Hill, Oxford OX2 8EJ
OXFORD   LONDON   EDINBURGH
MADRID   ATHENS   BOLOGNA   PARIS
MELBOURNE   SYDNEY   AUCKLAND
IBADAN   NAIROBI   HARARE   GABORONE
SINGAPORE   TOKYO   PORSTMOUTH NH (USA)

ISBN 0 435 12243 6

94 95 15 14 13 12 11 10 9 8 7 6

Printed in England by Clays Ltd, St Ives plc

CONTENTS

Skulker Wheat   1

Gaffer Roberts   8

Chunny's Pig   16

A Miracle   22

George Cummings   29

The Twenty Pound Bike   39

Baron Warthead   46

Wobble-Gob   53

Dumpy Cackitt   59

Dick   65

The Football Pools Winner   74

Skulker Wheat

Skulker Wheat had a face shaped like a blackbird's egg. It was long, pointed and crammed full of big brown freckles. I used to go birds' nesting with Skulker, Jud Price, Woolly Lamb and Fatty Heathershaw. Fatty was a big, fat boy of fourteen and he was our leader; he knew where all the unusual nests were: barn owls', blue tits' and even a corncrake's. The rest of us used to tramp along behind Fatty, having great faith in his knowledge of the nesting habits of skylarks, robins and bummy wrens but, as we were only eight and Fatty was fourteen, we were always convinced that the next old water pump or tumbled-down barn would yield an amazing nest, crammed with hundreds of red and green eggs.

Of course we were often delayed by Skulker; he had fits. We would be walking in single file along a hedgerow, all peering intently into the thickest parts for the tell-tale straw or twigs, when someone would notice that Skulker was missing. He would be about a hundred yards adrift, having a fit. Skulker always had his fits standing up. He would stand stock-still except for his head which would jerk backward and forward like an agitated blackbird on its nest. His fits would only last about two minutes but two minutes were an age when you were in pursuit of a pied-wagtail's nest which was just around the corner. (Fatty had seen it last night when he was out for a walk with his ferret.)

One day Skulker's fit seemed to be lasting longer than usual and we all stood around him, impatiently looking into his glazed eyes to see if he was coming out of it. Suddenly

1

Woolly Lamb gave him a push. Skulker fell over and started to kick around like a dog with colic; then he started to foam at the mouth and make funny noises like someone having a bad dream.

'You shouldn't push him, Woolly. Now look what you've done. I'm telling Big Bonzo about you.'

Big Bonzo was Skulker's uncle. Well, he wasn't his proper uncle. He was billeted in Skulker's house during the war and afterwards came back and lived there permanently. There were quite a lot of them lived in Skulker's house but I know one of the women living there must have been Skulker's mother because she looked like Skulker. Also one day when Woolly and I had gone to call for Skulker, this sharp-faced woman had said, 'My Billy's not coming out for a long time: I've locked him in his room.'

Woolly and I were wandering away when the top window of Skulker's council house opened suddenly. Skulker leaned right out and shouted, 'Woolly, Woolly don't tek no notice of the old goat.' Skulker was about to say more but his head disappeared even more suddenly than it had appeared and was replaced by Big Bonzo's. Woolly and I fled but I was pretty sure after that that the sharp-faced woman was Skulker's mother.

Skulker was still wriggling about a bit, but not quite so violently.

'Big Bonzo said to leave him alone when he had a fit; you heard him say it, Woolly. He'll hammer you.'

We were all a bit worried; Woolly was throwing stones into the hedge but he kept looking anxiously back at Skulker. Suddenly Skulker stopped wriggling. Jud Price approached him carefully and looked at his face.

'I reckon he's dead,' said Jud in a whisper. 'You've killed him Woolly.'

'See if he's breathing,' said Fatty, sitting down about twenty yards away from the prostrate Skulker.

2

'You can test him on a bit of glass,' I said.

I had a bit of an old mirror in my pocket—I had a bit of everything in my pocket in those days—and I threw it to Jud. He picked it up and approached Skulker cautiously.

'What shall I do with it?' he asked.

'Put it under his nose; see if it goes misty.'

As Jud placed the glass—wrong way up—on Skulker's spotty nose Skulker suddenly sat bolt upright. Jud gave a quick sharp scream and sat down.

'What's up with you?' said Skulker.

'Nothing,' said Jud, slipping the piece of glass into his pocket.

We all set off after a bullfinch nest but only Skulker said anything. Woolly soon said his tea would be ready and went home.

It was Skulker's real metal catapult that finally caused his downfall. We all had catapults made from a forked stick. We were for ever pulling branches out of hedges that looked suitable for catty prongs. The bottom part of the 'Y' had to be thicker than its two arms; the arms had to be the same thickness as each other and about three inches apart. Of course you had to buy the catty elastic from Woolies' and make a sling out of a bit of old saddle or something.

We didn't hit much with our catties. Occasionally someone might knock a few feathers out of an old, slow-witted sparrow. But usually we used to shoot old birds' nests out of the hedge—not new ones because we ... well anyway we didn't shoot new ones. As we were patrolling a hedge someone, usually Fatty, would shout, 'Next, baggy fuggy.'

'Seggy,' 'Firdy,' 'Forf,' and occasionally, usually me, 'Fifth,' would come the shouts in quick succession. No sooner had precedence for the ownership of the eggs been established in this manner—it often led to fights—when Fatty would shout, 'Laggy's,' and we all started to curse

3

and out would come the catties. Sometimes it would take as long as twenty minutes to shoot the old bird's nest out of the hedge and often I was delegated to struggle through the brambles and pull it out. We never left one; we felt it had cheated us, promising eggs or at least 'yunkers' and turning out to have nothing in it except a few of last year's leaves.

So, when Skulker turned up with this real metal catapult, we were all pretty impressed; not that we let on though. He'd got some thick black elastic to go with it and a real leather sling.

'Where'd you get it?' asked Jud.

'Our Jack bought it in Mansfield.' Skulker always called Big Bonzo 'Jack'.

'I'll get my Dad to fetch me one,' said Jud. Jud's Dad could speak thirteen languages and was very rich. I often wondered if learning so many languages had made him stutter—once when I had asked him if Jud was coming out, it took him about ten minutes to say no.

'They're only made in this special shop in Mansfield,' said Skulker.

'I bet my Dad'll get one,' said Jud, but without much conviction in his voice.

'Let's have a go,' said Woolly, sounding casual. Skulker had thought of that one.

'Jack says I'm not to let anybody have a go or he'll take it off me.'

'He won't know; he's not here.'

'No, you've got your own. I ain't letting you have a go.'

'Let's have a look then.'

'Give us it straight back then.'

'OK.'

Woolly took the catapult and examined it critically. He pulled back the elastic and sighted an imaginary bird.

' 'Ere, give us it back; you're 'aving a go with it.'

'I ain't got a stone in it, have I?'

4

'Give us it.'

Skulker snatched back the catty and put it in his trouser's pocket. We walked on in silence, each of us planning to get a go with Skulker's catty.

'I'll be able to knock off a few birds now,' said Skulker.

'What, you!' said Woolly scornfully. 'You couldn't hit that water-trough last week from five yards.'

It was true. Skulker was the worst shot of us all. Once he had a fit while he was aiming at a water-hen. He held the catty rigid until his fit passed. Just as he was coming out he let go and the water-hen gave a squawk as the stone hit its tail. That was the best shot Skulker ever did and he didn't even know he was doing it.

'Bet I'll get a bird before Sat'day,' said Skulker and, as we were all slightly in awe of the metal catty, none of us contradicted him.

For the next month Skulker shot at every bird in the ornithologist's year book. He started with the little ones— just to give them a chance—but as he grew more desperate he shot at anything in sight. Once he nearly got a one-legged crow that was caught in the bottom of a bramble bush but it wriggled out before he could get his third shot at it and flew away cackling scornfully. But that was the nearest to success he came. In the end he got his ear clipped by old Chunny James for shooting at her Rhode Island Red hen which she kept in a run in her backyard.

The more Skulker missed the more we pleaded with him for a go. We were each quite sure that with the metal catty we could knock a zig-zagging swallow out of the sky first stone. But the more despairing Skulker became the more determined he was not to let anyone else touch his catty. I think he felt that we would get something straight-away and make a fool of him.

When nesting time arrived we began our daily prowls round the thickest hedgerows in the area. We were just about to pack up one night when Jud spotted a blackbird sitting on its nest in a solitary hawthorn bush. It was down-wind of us and facing away so it didn't hear or see us as we all gathered round Jud and peered at it. Jud's head was only about a yard away from the black feathers of its tail. I think the same idea occurred to all of us at the same time: we could catch it. Old Broddy Davies had a tame white blackbird called Rupert; we used to feed it with bread and spit in its mouth when it was thirsty. Perhaps it was the desire to own a tame blackbird that made us all want to catch it. Woolly put out his grubby hand, but Jud motioned him away. He was the nearest and he began to inch his hand towards the black unmoving feathers. But while his hand was still six inches away the blackbird's head suddenly disappeared. It didn't make any noise but the head just wasn't there any more.

'Got it,' said Skulker, with a grin of triumph on his mottled face, and he put his catty back into his pocket.

None of us said anything but Fatty lifted the dead black-bird off its nest and dropped it into the bottom of the hedge. Underneath it four young blackbirds, feathers half-grown, lifted their heads and opened their gaping mouths for food.

We turned away and trudged silently home. Even Skulker seemed subdued but just as we were climbing the last stile, he started a fit. He was in front of the stile step and Woolly couldn't get past. Woolly paused for a moment and then gave Skulker an almighty shove. He fell forward, hit his head on the stile step and rolled on to the floor. He started to foam and kick a bit but this time nobody took any notice of him. We just walked home and left him to his fit.

I suppose he must have got home all right because we used to see him about. But we never had much to do with him for a long time after that. He died about two years later. His fits got worse and in the end he had a really big one and never recovered.

6

Our Mams made us go to the funeral. We sat huddled together at the back of the cold, gloomy old church in our best suits and with serious faces. Then four men came struggling in through the door carrying Skulker in a big yellow-looking coffin. After him came his ginger Mam, holding on to Big Bonzo and blubbering away so that you could hear her all round the church. We were embarrassed and Woolly and I knelt down and pretended to say a prayer, like you have to when you first come into church.

The four blokes carrying Skulker put him down at the front and then stood in the first row of the pews. They were from the undertaker's in the town six miles away and they'd come especially to bury Skulker. There was another one of them; I think he was in charge because after old Parson Percy had said a few prayers they all struck up singing 'Abide with me'. The one in charge stood behind the four singing and kept looking at them; I think they were paid according to how much noise they made.

After that we took Skulker out and put him in his grave. Jud threw a handful of muck in on to his coffin lid like all the others did. It made a sharp clunking noise as it hit the wood because Jud had picked up a stone in his handful of muck. I noticed it because it was quite a big round stone and I couldn't help thinking it would have been a good one to shoot in a catty.

Gaffer Roberts

If my Mam got mad with me for something I'd done—or more often something I hadn't done—she used to make moaning noises and stagger about the house as if she was dying. My Dad used to say, 'Now look what you've done to your mother,' and if I answered back, he would start pelting things at me—plates, cups, his dinner, the carving knife, and once a picture of Jesus floating up to heaven with a lamb tucked under each arm.

When he started his pelting I ran, either to my bedroom upstairs or to the toilet at the bottom of the garden. Both places had latches and as long as I got ten yards' start on him, I could slam the door shut and slip my half clothes-peg under the latch—I always carried a half clothes-peg for the purpose—and no matter how much he blasphemed and kicked at the door he couldn't get in.

One Monday morning I lay in bed looking out of my skylight window at nothing in particular; there wasn't anything to see except sky because the window was merely a hole in the roof which you could open or shut with a long wooden handle. I had to sleep with it closed because if I left it open the cat would jump in and more likely than not land from ten feet on to my face—a nasty way to wake up. Anyway this particular Monday morning I didn't feel like getting up although my Mam had already shouted: 'If he thinks he's going to have me at his beck and call just to get him his breakfast when he wants, he's got another think coming.' She never addressed me directly when she was mad.

When I eventually got downstairs she said to my Dad,

'Tell him his breakfast's in the oven if he wants it.' I was feeling pretty fed up but I shouldn't have said what I did.

'Tell her to stuff her head in the oven.'

I know it wasn't very witty but it certainly galvanized my Dad.

'Right you great wammock,' he shouted and looked round for something to pelt. I was still a bit sleepy and I hesitated a moment, not knowing whether to run to the bog or the bedroom. The last time I'd made for the bog he'd broken my back when he caught me straight between the shoulder blades with a loaf of bread. If you think that wouldn't hurt, I'd better tell you it was one of Albert Rowe's specials —stale and very crusty.

Anyway that thought decided me to make for the bedroom but I was late starting and had only just reached the top of the stairs when he was half-way up with the big brown teapot held in his pelting position. I wasn't going to make it! I couldn't possibly get the peg in the door before he got his foot in it. I turned to face him. He stopped. Neither of us knew what to do. Then he put his head down, growled and took the last few stairs three at a time. Just as he reached the top step I gave him a push—not a hard push, just defensive. He lost his balance and he and the teapot clattered downstairs. He reached the bottom first and the teapot, a close second, hit him on the head and smashed, spilling luke-warm tea down his navy-blue shirt. He looked up at me with a scowl, a scowl of surprise. I looked down at him in astonishment. It was a significant moment. Neither of us spoke. He picked up the broken pot and went away.

After that he still chased me, firing away with Wellington boots, sugar bowls and other unlikely weapons. But both of us knew he didn't intend catching me. We both went a bit slower. What used to be a real chase had become a ritual. I had become as strong as my Dad.

I'm telling you all this about my Dad because in a

9

peculiar way it helps to explain in my mind the downfall of Gaffer Roberts.

I used to hate meeting Gaffer Roberts when I was a boy. Even before I was five he used to plague me with questions. I would be walking home with my Dad after singling beet or something and meet Gaffer coming out of school. He was headmaster of the village school, a matchstick man with a bent back—as if one of the matches had slipped forward— and a rusty face; he had some disease that made his skin go rusty.

'Afternoon, Fred,' Gaffer would say to my Dad.

'Afternoon, suh,' my Dad would say.

'So this is the youngster, is it Fred? Let's see, how old will he be now?'

I always managed to tell him my age but that was about the limit of my side of the conversation with Gaffer.

'Now, young man, I've got a sixpence, a threepenny bit and six pennies in my pocket. How much does that make?'

When Gaffer first asked me that sort of question I thought he was bragging about his wealth so I said, 'Very good,' or something like that, but I noticed it didn't go down very well. Later I learnt that no sums teacher can ask you a straightforward question. They always have to go on about Bill Smith setting out to walk somewhere or Joe Brown filling his bath, instead of just asking the volume of water in a container. I think it's supposed to make it more interesting having Joe Browns and Bill Smiths in it.

I got very few of Gaffer's sums right. The more he asked the worst I got. It was his head that put me off, when he bent down to ask his questions. You see he'd only got a big tuft of black hair in the middle of his head but he used it carefully, spreading it out from the centre to all parts of his head and keeping it plastered down with Brylcreem. As there wasn't enough to cover his head properly he had wide partings to disguise his baldness. Two wide partings ran from front to back and two from side to side. When

10

he bent down to ask me questions his head just looked as if it had been set out for a game of noughts and crosses. And that's what put me off! When he started on about his half-crowns in his waistcoat I tried to concentrate, but I just couldn't stop myself playing mental noughts and crosses on his head. Once I beat myself and got a row of noughts down the right hand side of his head and I gave myself a small grin of triumph.

'There's nothing to laugh at young man,' said Gaffer in a nasty way, as if he'd been saying things like 'Wipe that grin off your face' for years. 'You'll find a sound basic knowledge of mathematics essential for life, essential.' Gaffer emphasized the point by tapping me on the head.

My Dad was mad with me when Gaffer had match-sticked his way down the road.

'It's a pity he's retiring; he'd sort you and the rest of the young devils out, would old Gaffer. He nearly killed your Uncle Jack with a walking-stick because he was late for school one morning.'

My Dad went on and on about how fierce Old Gaffer was and how there ought to be more teachers like him about.

'He's only sixty-two; he's still got a lot of life in him. Nobody messed about in Gaffer's school.'

I was surprised Gaffer was only sixty-two; he looked more like a hundred and sixty-two to me, but I was quite impressed by what my Dad said about him and whenever I saw Gaffer after that I tried to hide so that he didn't see me. I was pretty scared of him.

It was several years later and I was in the top class at the village school. Fatty Heathershaw, Woolly Lamb and Skulker were in the same class despite being older than me. You see if you didn't pass to go to the school in town you stayed at the village school until you were fourteen. We were a pretty rowdy lot and the Headmaster, Silas Rudkin, had a job to keep us in order. One morning he ran off with the dinner and bank money. He didn't get very far—to his sister's in Newark—so the police found him by Friday and got most of the thirty pounds back. It was then that they gave out that he'd had what they called a nervous breakdown and that it was caused by 'pressure of work'. I didn't know whether we were the 'pressure of work' but I'm sure we must have been part of it at least.

They couldn't get a new teacher for the next few weeks so they got Gaffer to come out of his retirement. The Vicar came to tell us the news just before we went home on Friday. I wasn't very pleased and neither were most of the others. We all knew Gaffer's reputation and felt we had to be on our best behaviour.

The first three days all went quite well. We sat and listened to Old Gaffer going on about verbs and Pythagoras and capital towns. It was a good job Old Gaffer's reputation was so strong because he was even more boring than Silas Rudkin.

'Please, sir,' said Skulker on the Thursday morning when Gaffer was going on about tin-mining in Bolivia, 'can I go to the toilet?'

'Yes, I suppose you are able to,' said Gaffer with a sarcastic grin. Skulker got up and shambled to the door.

'Where are you going boy?'

'To the toilet, sir.'

'I said I presumed you were able to go to the toilet. If you are asking my permission to go the answer is no, certainly not.' Gaffer sat back with a grin of triumph on his face.

None of us had a clue what he was talking about and the next half-hour he bored us silly going on about the difference between 'can' and 'may' and smirking all the time as if he'd outsmarted us.

At break we turned on Skulker, saying it was his fault for asking to go to the toilet. Skulker didn't see that it was his fault; neither did we actually but as we daren't get at

12

Gaffer Roberts we had to blame somebody and Skulker seemed the best target. In the end Skulker said, 'I'll fix him after break.'

We sneered at this; Skulker only dared to muck about when everybody else was. This time we had underestimated him though.

After break Gaffer started on measuring fields in acres and rods and that sort of thing.

'A farmer wants to plant a field of wheat,' said Gaffer, 'but he doesn't know how much seed to buy. So he goes into the field and starts to measure down one side in yards. The first side measures. . . .'

'What if there's a bull in it?' shouted Skulker. There was a frozen silence. I looked at Skulker with interest, wondering what sort of corpse he would make and how long it would take to clear the blood up. I think we were all amazed, even Skulker, when Old Gaffer pretended not to hear him and picked up the thread of his sum.

'Down the first side he measures eighty-seven yards,' said Gaffer, 'and down the next side he measures. . . .'

'Yes, but what if there's a bull in the field?' shouted Skulker, so loudly that he couldn't be ignored.

Gaffer put down his chalk. 'This is it!' I thought. 'We'll have to find a new goalkeeper for the football team.' Skulker was a rotten goalie anyway doing great acrobatic dives after the ball was in the net.

'Who are you boy?'

'Wheat,' said Skulker in a hoarse whisper.

'Come here, Wheat. I'm going to have to thrash you.' Skulker didn't move.

'Come here,' shouted Old Gaffer in a loud but panicky sort of voice. Skulker sat down.

Then Gaffer went towards him and suddenly started clipping Skulker round the ears and hair with both hands. But it was obvious from the start that he wasn't hurting Skulker at all. After about a minute Old Gaffer was breathing heavily; he was about all in. He went back and sat in his chair.

Nothing more was said that lesson but the writing was on the wall for Old Gaffer. Next morning we had Religious Knowledge. Each boy had to read a verse from the Bible one after the other round the form. Well, Fatty Heathershaw started reading his verse. When he'd finished I started mine; the only trouble for Old Gaffer was that Fatty started to read his again and when I'd finished Woolly started his and Fatty and I started ours again. It was quite easy if you kept your head down and concentrated on reading your verse louder than anybody else. As the noise and babble increased Old Gaffer started to shout, 'Stop, stop it at once,' but soon he couldn't make himself heard. He started to run up and down the rows shouting into each boy's ear, telling him to stop. When he did this you stopped for a few seconds and then started up again when he went further down the row. With Silas Rudkin we'd got up to fifteen people reading different verses at once, until he managed to stop us by hitting each of the readers on the head with a metal ruler.

With Old Gaffer we got twenty-two reading before the bell rang for break. That stopped us.

'You louts, you fools, you wait,' was all Gaffer managed to say.

'You said each one read a verse,' shouted Woolly. Gaffer got up and walked out. Friday was fairly quiet after that. We knew we'd won and didn't want to make a fuss about it; after all he was an old bloke.

He didn't turn up the next Monday and old Mrs Armitage had us with her class. We got on all right there. She wasn't too bad and we didn't muck about. I don't know why we didn't muck about with her. We just didn't; we didn't seem to want to annoy her somehow.

Old Gaffer didn't come back again and I began to feel sorry for him. But after a time I felt it served him right.

If you scare people by hitting them then one day they'll be able to get you; it stands to reason. Anyway, he shouldn't have been sarcastic and smart; him and his 'may I' and 'can I' and all that clever nonsense.

Chunny's Pig

Every Monday I went pig-killing with my Dad and my
Uncle Dick. We usually killed about five and cut them up
in the afternoon. We charged a pound for killing the pig
and ten bob for cutting it up. When I say killing a pig,
I don't just mean killing it. There was a lot more to do
than just cutting its throat; that was the easy bit. Well, it
was usually the easy bit, except in the case of Nob Hill's
Dad's pig.

You see everybody in our village kept a pig. If you were
poor you shared a pig with a neighbour. When the pig was
cut up you used to pack salt round it in a big wooden
trough and after a few weeks you hung the bits of pig all
round the living room walls. They were like pictures
nowadays, except you kept cutting bits off to keep you
going through the winter.

In case you don't know how to kill a pig, I'll tell you.
At about eight o'clock on Monday morning we would set
off in our old green Commer van, Uncle Dick driving, my
Dad in the passenger seat smoking Digger Flake and me
sitting in the scalding tub in the back of the van surrounded
by knives, scrapers, skewers and the cratch—all the tackle
needed to kill a pig. The first thing you do when you arrive
is to check that they've got the copper boiling. You need
about ten buckets of boiling water to kill a pig, and if the
copper isn't boiling my Uncle Dick gets mad.

I remember when we went to kill Chunny James's pig
one year and her water wasn't even warm. Uncle Dick
stomped round Chunny's yard in his Wellington boots

smoking his Craven A fags and wiping his nose on his apron
—he always wore a blue apron for killing a pig. Anyway
he'd smoked five fags before the copper boiled; it took him
a long time to smoke a fag too because he used to stick a pin
in the end so he could smoke every shred of tobacco.

When the copper was boiling at last, my Dad and me
went to catch Chunny's pig. Chunny's sty was at the bottom
of her garden so we thought we'd kill the pig near the sty
and carry it back to the yard on the cratch—the cratch was
like the stretcher you see them carrying people who have
fainted out of football grounds, only bigger, because pigs
are bigger than people I suppose.

Chunny's pig was a sixteen-stoner with a black stripe
down its back. I knew it would take a lot of killing as soon
as I saw it and the black stripe was a nuisance too. Black
bristles took much more scraping off than white ones.

As soon as we looked over the sty at Chunny's pig, it stood
up, grunted and went through the hole at the end of its
sty into the small section where it slept. It didn't think we
were going to kill it or anything; it probably didn't like the
look of Uncle Dick who had joined us by now and was
coughing and spitting on account of smoking too many
fags. I sympathized with Chunny's pig; I didn't like the
look of my Uncle Dick either. He had greasy black hair, a
pasty face and never smiled.

'See if you can get the rope on it, boy. If you can't, just
drive it out.'

I was only about seven so I could get through the hole
easily. Chunny's pig was sitting on its straw looking a bit
fierce. The rope was about ten feet long with a loop at the
end. You had to get the loop between its teeth—like a bit
in a horse's mouth—and then pull it tight. I crawled up to
the pig and slowly dangled the loop on its snout. It did a
very stupid thing then, did Chunny's pig. It bit at the
loop and that was just what I wanted and I pulled the
rope tight. It got up and pulled me through the gap into

17

the main part of the sty. I probably looked like a midget trying to take an Alsatian for a walk.

'Good lad,' said my Dad when he saw I was still holding the rope. I didn't tell him it was a fluke. Then we walked the pig round the side of the sty where we were going to kill it.

I ought to tell you that sometimes we shot pigs before we stuck them, but some old folks in the village, such as Chunny, didn't like them shot first because they thought it sent the meat bad. My Dad was good at stabbing pigs after they'd been shot and were lying down, but Uncle Dick was best at stabbing them when they were standing up.

Well, we pushed Chunny's pig against the wall of the sty and my Dad got hold of its tail in his left hand and pushed his whole weight against its body so it couldn't back away. My job was to pull its head up with the rope and as soon as I'd done this Uncle Dick cut its throat with a quick upward thrust of his nine-inch knife. As soon as I pulled on the rope Chunny's pig started screaming like a ... well I've never heard anything scream half so loud as a stuck pig.

It seemed that one second there was Uncle Dick's black hairy bare arm with a clean shining knife in his hand and the next second everything was covered in blood. Dick's arm and apron and even his Wellington boots were thick red. We held the pig upright till most of its blood was gone. At least Chunny didn't stand around holding basins and tins to catch the blood to make black puddings like some of them did. That was always a nuisance—they used to get in your way.

The screaming gave way to grunts and Chunny's pig flopped on to its side; but it wasn't dead yet. You had to pump the rest of the blood out of the hole in its throat by lifting its fore-leg up and down. My Dad did this for a bit and in about five minutes the pig was properly dead. You

18

could test it by putting a trickle of boiling water in its ear. If it didn't flap its ear it was dead.

Then we rolled the pig on the cratch and I took the bloodied rope from its mouth. Uncle Dick and Dad then staggered up the path carrying the pig and I ran on to get the scalding trough as near to the copper as I could. I set it up outside Chunny's back door. It was wooden and shaped like a half-barrel but about four feet across and two feet deep with tar on the outside to stop the water running out. By the time Dad and Dick arrived with the pig I'd already got the first two buckets of boiling water in the scalding trough.

Just then Old Chunny came out with three cups of tea and a few biscuits on a tray. The cups had dainty flower patterns but no saucers and the biscuits were digestive; she was trying to make up for not having her copper boiling but the poor old devil was only making things worse. You didn't have time to drink tea when you'd got a dead pig to scald. You had to get its bristles off before its body went cold. Uncle Dick just grunted at her but my Dad said, 'No thanks, Mrs James. We'd like a drink after though.'

Chunny looked a bit disappointed and hobbled off with her tray.

Ten buckets of water in the tub and in went the pig's head and shoulders. Then we picked up our scrapers and worked like madmen. A scraper looks like a big mushroom but with a sharp metal rim round the top. We scraped away at Chunny's pig, the hairs coming away in wet lumps. After about two minutes we turned the pig over and scraped the other side; then turned it round and put its behind in the water.

In about ten minutes the pig was on the cratch looking quite clean. We got our knives out then and scraped off the rest of the hairs, dipping our knives in the water every now and then to clean them. When Uncle Dick was satisfied that there were no more hairs to cut off—I'd cut through its skin twice trying to get the black hairs out of its back and Dick scowled at me and I thought he was going to clip my ear—we put the pig on its back on the cratch and tied its back legs to the handles. Then we propped it up, head down, against the wall of Chunny's house.

Uncle Dick slit the pig from top to bottom with his killing knife and took out its insides. He staggered off with his arms full of pig's guts and dropped them all in the scalding tub—I'd tipped the water and hair away down Chunny's drain. Dick then cut out the liver and heart and dropped them into a clean bucket of water; this was pig's fry and Chunny might give us a bit to take back for our suppers.

I knew what my job was now and I didn't like it. There was about three miles of pig's intestines in the scalding tub and I had to find the end and run the whole lot through my fingers. I didn't mind it too much until I got near the end. Then all the pig muck started coming out over my boots and it used to stink something horrible. It had to be done though because we needed the insides to make sausages with—we had them properly cleaned though before we put sausage meat in them.

When I'd finished that nasty job I had to go and pull the pig's toe nails off with a metal hook. Sometimes you could hurt yourself doing that; you'd get the hook in the nail and pull and pull and suddenly it would give and over you'd go smack on your backside.

I managed to do it easy though with Chunny's pig and when I'd finished my jobs I went to my Dad and asked him for the bladder. Uncle Dick had just finished cutting off its head and he dropped it upside down in another bucket. My Dad had saved me the bladder and I blew it up and tied the end with a piece of binder-twine.

Then I played football with it round Chunny's yard till it burst—they didn't last long. When I got back I was just in time to help swill down. We chucked a few buckets of cold water over the pig and washed the rest of the blood and hair down the drain. My Dad loaded the tackle in the van and I buried the rest of the insides in the garden while Dick went to get the money from Chunny.

We hadn't time for tea after all because we were late already and Walter Worthington's copper would have boiled dry if we weren't quick.

Anyway that's how we killed Chunny's pig and that's how we killed hundreds of pigs when I was a boy. I hope you didn't think it was cruel the way we killed pigs. I certainly would do now but I didn't think about it then; I just grew up with it, I suppose.

A Miracle

Do you believe in miracles? I didn't until I was eight, and then one happened to me and my mates at the Village Garden Fête. It was held every July on the vicar's lawn. He had about half an acre of lawn; it was proper lawn as well, all short and green like they play bowls on nowadays, not scrubby old rye grass full of holes and dandelions like the rest of the villagers had. He had a great big house as well, did our vicar, full of hidden rooms and long dark passages that we only explored properly a few years later when we went to confirmation classes. My Dad used to say he had a pretty good set up considering he only worked one day a week; but to be fair he used to do other things as well, such as being scorer for the cricket team.

He certainly worked hard at the fête. He pranced about in his pin-striped suit, his long horse-face beaming away at all the people trying to put up the side-shows and the marquees.

About two o'clock he stood on a chair and made a speech; we only ever listened once but it was the same every year. It was all about the charities that would benefit from the profit on the fête, most of it to buy dogs for the blind men. I wondered if they'd buy a dog for old Arthur Drury to help him find the right pew in church, because a few weeks ago when I'd joined the choir again, just before the choir outing to Skegness, old Arthur came tapping away with his white stick and sat himself down in the front pew. The vicar shifted him out just in time before Lady Roberts came. She would have been mad to find old Arthur in her special front pew.

Anyway, after the vicar had finished his speech we set off round the stalls. We always had a go at Dick Price's table skittles first, before he got mad and changed the rules. The prize was always a dead duck and to win it you had to knock down the highest number of skittles on the day. There were nine skittles on the table, which was like an oblong shallow trough, with the front end open, and it stood on four legs. You had three cheeses—flat rubber circles about three inches across—and you didn't stand much chance unless you knocked all nine down with your first two cheeses. Then Dick used to stand the skittles up again so you could throw your last cheese at a full table of skittles. Fourteen or fifteen knocked down would have a good chance of winning.

There were two ways of getting a good score. First was to have your mates near the table so that when you threw your cheese someone could give the back a nudge and knock all the skittles down. Dick wasn't a very bright bloke but he knew something was wrong when Woolly Lamb threw his cheese, missed the table altogether and all the skittles fell down. After that Dick always used to say, 'Clear the table,' and we had to stand at least two yards away before he would allow anyone to throw.

There was a better way of cheating though. The table had wobbly legs and if you hit the board at the back with your cheese the vibration would bring down all the skittles. You had to pelt the cheese really hard to do this though and it only worked for a couple of years.

When he saw what was happening Dick said that you had to flick the cheese out of the back of your hand. Of course you couldn't get the same force that way so you had to rely on having a sly wang when Dick's concentration lapsed.

On the afternoon of the miracle we'd got a new plan. There was this old boy called Ernie Hobson with us; he was eight but was stunted and only looked about five. He lived right down the bottom of Church Hill so Dick didn't know him. We'd practised him in what to do. He bought his three cheeses for twopence and stood on the white-wash line about six feet from the table. Then he did a couple of very feeble, back-hand flicks, so feeble that they didn't reach the table.

'Oh, Dick, look at that poor old boy.'

'What's up?'

'He can't reach the table; he's only four. Let him pelt 'em.'

'He can come a bit nearer.'

We hadn't bargained for this but Ernie was quite a bright lad and even at the new distance he managed to make it look as if he couldn't reach the table.

'Let him have another go and pelt 'em, Dick. I think he's nearly roaring.'

'All right,' said Dick, scared at the possibility of tears.

Ernie was really a good pelter and his first cheese hit the back of the table with a thump and down came all the skittles. He scored seventeen—an almost certain winner.

'That's cheered him up, Dick.'

'Scab off,' said Dick, thinking he'd been made a fool of.

'We'll be back about five for the duck, Dick,' I said and we went off to our favourite stall—Nutty Hobbins' darts.

Well, it wasn't darts really. There was a sort of dart-board on a post but you could spin it round like a Catherine wheel. It was divided into about ten segments, the biggest segment marked 'Woodbine' and the smallest 'Cigar'. All the other segments had names of cigarettes marked on them. They were all different sizes. You spun the board and someone threw a dart at it. Of course, it had the best chance of landing in the biggest segment so the odds against Woodbine were only 2-1; cigar was 20-1. Near the dart-board was a table divided into ten squares; the name of the cigarette and its odds were marked in each square. You put the money on the square of your choice. It was a sort of poor man's roulette, I suppose. I think the game was funnier than roulette though. Skulker Wheat used to put a penny on every square. He said he was bound to win that way. When he'd lost all his money he used to start advising the rest of us.

There wasn't any way you could cheat fairly on Nutty's darts. One or two used to move their money after the board had stopped revolving but you couldn't do it very easily and anyway it was a rotten trick. The funny part was throwing the dart. There was always a big crowd round Nutty and about half of them wanted a go at throwing.

'Let's have a throw, Nutty.'

'No, it's my turn; I asked ages ago, Nutty.'

'It's right, he did, boy,' Nutty said, looking worried.

'He's a liar, Nutty, he's only just come. Give us the dart.'

You can imagine in such a situation there were some very bad throwers. If Skulker got hold of the dart, you ducked. He was useless. He made it worse by shutting one eye and trying to sight out 'Cigar' or something while the board was flashing round at twenty miles an hour. He usually missed the board altogether. Sometimes there were as many as four misses in a row; then Nutty would get mad and rush to the front.

'Give us 'old that bleeding dart, boy,' he would shout and savagely hurl it in before the board stopped revolving.

The real trouble though was if the dart hit the wire between the segments. It would fly off at any angle and could do you a nasty injury. You knew if it hit the wire by the pinging noise it made; then you ducked quickly or dropped on the floor.

Two years ago a very funny thing happened. Fatty Heathershaw threw the dart very hard and there was a loud ping. Everybody ducked and three or four people fell in a heap behind the table. Nutty was one of them, and he was the last up.

'Are you all right, Nutty?' asked Woolly.

25

Nutty stood up and looked about him.

'Yes, I'm all right, boy. But where's the bloody dart?'

The dart was stuck straight between Nutty's eyes, just above the bridge of his nose. He looked like a unicorn. The dart had gone into Nutty so fast that he hadn't yet felt the pain.

Nothing funny happened this year on Nutty's stall though, so we walked round having a go at looping rings over bottles with a fishing rod, and finding buried treasure by sticking little white markers in the ground.

When it was time for the auction to start we went into the big marquee to look round as usual. Every year they had this auction of all the things that the shop-keepers and richer folks in the village had given. A proper auctioneer always came from the neighbouring town and the vicar made his usual speech about how kind Mr Perkins was to offer his services free. He didn't look very kind to me. His face was a bit redder than ever though and he'd grown even fatter. They had some smashing things to auction as usual; huge tins of sweets, great baskets of fruit and even things like bikes and footballs. Not that we could ever buy anything. The prices they paid were fantastic, even more than you would have to pay in the shop. This was because old Perkins and the vicar kept on about worthy causes the money was going to help.

We crowded to the front as usual but without the slightest hope of buying anything, especially as we'd only about a bob each left. We always had a bid though. The vicar passed this huge tin of toffees to Mr Perkins to start the auction.

'Now, who's going to start the bidding today, ladies and gentlemen?'

'Tanner,' said Skulker Wheat.

It was then that the miracle started to happen.

'Sold,' said Perkins in a loud voice and banged his hammer hard on the lid of the toffee tin.

Skulker was so surprised it took him about two minutes

to find his sixpence. He handed it to the vicar who smiled at him but looked a bit surprised. Skulker snatched his toffees and sat on them. Even then he didn't look as if he could believe his luck.

An assistant pushed a shining blue bike, with a dynamo and proper gears up to Perkins.

'And now,' said Perkins swaying a bit as he came from behind the table to take hold of the bike. 'Now what am I bid for this extremely magnificent bike?'

'Threepence,' said Fatty Heathershaw, just before Woolly, me and greedy Skulker.

'Sold,' said Perkins in an even louder voice than before and he banged his hammer on the bike's bell. It made such a good noise he did it again, several times, and rang the bell with his finger and laughed in a high-pitched voice.

This time the vicar's smile was a bit sickly as he handed Fatty the bike.

In the next ten minutes we used up all our money; but never had we used money to better purpose. I had a box of chocolates, a hedge-knife and a sledge for one and four-pence. Most of my other mates had done even better.

'Let's go home and get some more money,' said Woolly in an awed whisper.

But instinctively I knew it could not last. In fact things were happening already. People were rustling and whispering to each other.

'He's blind drunk,' I heard Brothy Davies say behind me.

'Proper canned,' Bert Price agreed.

I wasn't sure myself. I'd seen Sep Ramsden drunk and he was lying in the gutter puking all over his jacket and groaning. Old Perkins didn't look as if he was going to puke, but I suppose there are different ways of being drunk.

Then I noticed something else. Old Lady Roberts was passing stuff to the vicar at the back of the dais and the vicar was sneaking out the back of the marquee with it.

In another ten minutes the miracle was over.

'Everything's gone now, Mr Perkins,' said the vicar, a desperate, forced grin on his face. He needn't have worried, God didn't strike him dead and old Perkins had had enough.

'Yes, good, well, er, I'll be away then,' said old Perkins and jumped quickly off the dais and ran out of the marquee. He'd only gone to the corrugated-iron toilet under the bushes, though, and it was another half-hour before they had him in his car and he was driven home by Lady Roberts's chauffeur.

When we had finished seeing him off we went back to the tent and there was the vicar getting out all the things he'd hidden from old Perkins.

'Ladies and gentlemen,' said the vicar, standing on the dais, 'Mr Perkins has had a sudden indisposition. I'm sure you'll all agree that in the circumstances he was well-advised to return home and rest.' He looked very sheepish for a man with a horse's face.

'Lady Roberts has most kindly offered to continue the auction for us.'

There was a smattering of applause. 'But before she does,' he continued, 'I would like to make an appeal to the people who have bought items so far. In view of the importance of the charities we are supporting by this fête, I would ask people to consider giving ... er ... returning their articles for re-sale. They will, of course,' he nodded with a sickly grin, 'be reimbursed for any outlay they have made already.'

We didn't quite understand his long words, but we knew what he meant. We picked up our things and went out of the tent. Miracles only happen once in a lifetime.

George Cummings

Any old boy in our village could get a job at Wakefield's in the school holidays; even a kid of ten. I was ten when I first met George Cummings.

I went to see Master William and asked him for a job as soon as we broke up. Master William was Old Man Wakefield's son and Old Man Wakefield owned over a thousand acres, three-quarters of the land in the village. Old Man Wakefield only came out on pay-days though; he was ninety and Master William was sixty-three.

I crept cautiously up to Old Man Wakefield's house. The trouble was you didn't really know where to knock. The house was as long as Coronation Street and had about the same number of doors. All the windows were dark; you'd never guess anyone lived there. I went round the back and I was lucky because Master William was feeding his chickens.

'Please, Mr Wakefield, can I have a job?'

Master William turned round to look at me, a bucket in one hand and the chicken pellets in the other.

'Aren't you the young hooligan who killed my dog?'

'No, Mr Wakefield, it wasn't me.'

It wasn't either; it was Skulker Wheat. He was chasing a rabbit with a stick last summer and he was just about to hit it when Master William's whippet Rex nipped in to grab it with its mouth. Skulker couldn't stop his stick and Rex lay spreadeagled on the floor; the rabbit whipped back into the corn. We carried Rex back to Master William.

'Mr Wakefield, I think we've stunned your dog,' said Skulker.

'Stunned it! You've killed it you mean.'

Master William eventually believed me. 'You can go and work with old George Cummings mending fences in the forty-acre at the top of Pancake Hill. Be at the yard at seven sharp.'

I arrived at seven the next morning; the yard was deserted. At a quarter past the foreman Bill Morgan came slouching out of his cottage at the end of the yard.

'Who are you?' asked Bill, rubbing the sleep out of his eyes with his great red hands. I explained.

'Right,' said Bill, 'you go straight up to Pancake Hill. George'll go straight there. He won't come down here after that trouble about the nail in his hat. Whatever you do, boy, don't you say anything about the nail in his hat.'

I didn't dare ask why and I set off up Pancake Hill.

Pancake Hill had been made when a giant took a huge shovel full of muck to throw at Clifton Castle. He got half-way there when the shovel handle broke and the muck he spilt made Pancake Hill. That's what my Dad used to tell me anyway. I believed him till I was five.

I soon found old George. He was sitting under the hedge having his lunch. Lunch was what we call breakfast now; you had it when you'd been working about an hour. The first thing I thought about old George was that I didn't fancy his lunch; it was a lump of fat ten inches long. He was dipping one end into a can of milk and chewing it when it was well soaked. After he'd chewed up all the fat, he drank the milk, slurping it so that some dribbled down his chin and on to his old blue waistcoat. He had a greasy cheesecutter cap and sure enough the large tear in the top was held down by a rusty old four-inch nail.

When he had finished his lunch George stood up. He did it by stages; he was so old you expected him to creak like a five-barred gate as he straightened his skinny body.

'Come on, boy, I'll chop and you pull the bits into a pile.'

He seemed to know all about me so I said nothing and

followed him to the part of the hedge we were to lay. He was good with a hedge-knife, was old George. You had to thin the hedge out, like a barber thinning out your hair; but some bits you only had to cut half-way through so that you could twist them and lay them at an angle so that the hedge grew thick the next year.

I liked old George; I worked with him for a whole week on that hedge. He told me how when he first started farm-labouring he was paid seven pound a year and a new suit of clothes every Lady Day. He taught me how to catch a hare (if we saw one), set fire to a wet hedge and dig up a mole with a spade.

He was the bravest man I ever met. Just after dinner-time on the second day I worked with him, he was chopping away at some thick awkward brambles when his hedge-knife slipped and made a great six-inch gash in the top of his left hand. It started to bleed, not fast, but oozing up a sort of bluey-red colour. George looked at it a few seconds, then pulled out his box of matches from his pocket with his other hand. I had to hold the box while he struck a match. When the flame was steady he ran it slowly along the gash. He used three more matches before he was satisfied.

'That should seal it,' he said calmly, and within a few minutes he was chopping away at the hedge, using his good hand only, but almost as effectively as if he had two. If any of us had done that trick with a match we'd have been showing off—I'm sure none of us would dare to do it anyway. But I got the impression that George was just naturally tough.

George and I got on better and better as the week went on and we were quite good friends when we set off at half-past four on Friday to collect our wages. All the men were assembled in the yard when we got there. George didn't speak to them but went and sat on the stone trough and started to gouge out the black debris from the bowl of his pipe with an old black-handled pocket-knife. Two younger

blokes came across and stood over him. I knew one of them
—Septimus Ramsden; they called him that because he
was the seventh kid in their family. I didn't like him
because he had dropped my cricket bat down a well when
I wouldn't lend it to his scabby brother.

'Hello, George,' said Sep with a sarcastic grin on his
face. 'How's your nail?'

George didn't answer; he kept cleaning his pipe.

'You've made a real good job of that hat. Very neat
isn't it, Fred?' said Sep bringing his mate into the conversation.

'That's a left-handed pipe you got there, George. It'll
never work if you hold it like that.'

'Hey George, I can't start this tractor; the petrol's got
twisted up the pipe.'

They went on all stupid like this for a bit and in the end
they got old George mad. He didn't say anything; he just
picked up a hay-fork and made a stab at Sep. Sep and
Fred ran off shouting that Cummings was crackers. But
they weren't scared at all; it was just another way of
annoying old George.

George waved his fork at them and shouted something
about being in the trenches; I didn't catch what he said
because Old Man Wakefield's big black car made such a
row as it came into the stackyard. When it stopped we all
lined up outside the passenger window; Bill Morgan was
first because he was foreman. I stood at the back of the
line with old George. When it was George's turn he stood
by the window. Old Man Wakefield had a big red cash-box
on his knees. George took off his cap—the first time I'd seen
him without it—and as he bent down to the window I saw
knotted blue veins peeping out between the white wisps
of hair.

'Now then George,' said Old Man Wakefield.

'Normal week and three hours' overtime, Mr Wakefield,' said George.

'How much, Master William?' said Old Man Wakefield.

Master William was in the back seat with a big chart thing; he'd filled in all the hours each man had worked.

'Seven pounds sixteen, Father,' said Master William. Old Man Wakefield fumbled in the box and counted George's wages into his hat which he had pushed through the car window.

'Oh, George, you can give that roan cow a drink before you go. It's in the end box. You can take the old boy with you. We'd better give him his wages first though, eh?' said Old Man Wakefield and he cackled with laughter and spit fell into the box.

I didn't see what he was laughing at, especially when I got some of the money he had spat on after Master William had announced my wages to be three pounds, eight and fourpence.

Neither did I understand what giving a cow a drink was—I thought they could drink themselves—but I followed George to the box. The box was a shed about the size of a room in a house and in it was a large red and white cow chained by its neck to a manger. It was sick of something and the 'drink' was medicine we had to get down its throat. It didn't look very ill to me because it started to kick out with its hind legs, twist its neck and rattle its chain as soon as we squeezed our way into the box. It was a squeeze as well because the box seemed full of cow. George sidled round the side of the cow up to the manger. There was a shelf just above and on it was a pop bottle with milky-looking stuff in it. This was the drink.

I had no idea how we were going to make the cow drink its medicine. It didn't look the sort of cow that you could stick the bottle under its nose and say, 'Moo, moo, there's a good moo.' George pulled the cork out of the pop bottle and put his hand on the cow's head, saying, 'Whoa, there, whoa.' The cow lurched sideways and as its body came round it trapped George against the manger. It then gave him a kick with its hind legs and knocked him against the white-washed wall at the side of the box. George's head hit the wall and he sat down in a stunned heap, the cow's medicine dripping on to his old cord leggings. I ran out of the box and looked for someone to help and after five minutes of running round the stackyard I found no one; they'd all gone home. I went back to the box and peeped round the door. George was filling the bottle from the tap in the corner. He shook it to dissolve the white powder he had put in the bottom.

'Let's go home, George,' I said. George looked as if he needed medicine far more than the cow. His white hair was all bloody at the back and his face was pinched and white.

'We ain't going 'ome till we've drinked this bloody ol' cow,' said George. He didn't even sound mad; he said it as if he'd been knocked over by a cow every day.

'Get hold of its tail and twist it boy.'

'What?'

'It won't hurt you; get hold of its tail and give it a good twist when I've caught hold of its head.'

I approached the cow like someone trying to find his way through a dark room full of furniture. I kept my legs back and reaching forward with my right hand I grabbed the white tip of the cow's tail. George went up to the cow's head and suddenly pushed his thin old body against the cow's neck and pushed the head against the wall. He then thrust the thumb and forefinger of his right hand into the cow's wet nostrils and twisted its head round. I was so surprised that I forgot how scared I was, went nearer the cow and gave its tail a big twist with both hands. Unable to breathe through its nostrils the cow opened its mouth and George shoved the bottle down its throat. He must have got the neck of the bottle half-way down its windpipe because half his arm seemed to be in its mouth. There was a loud glugging sound for about ten seconds and then out

34

came George's arm, all slimy and with bloody fingers. We'd given the cow its drink.

'Are you all right, George?' I asked as we came out of the box into the safety of the stackyard.

'Course I am, boy; cows can't hurt you.'

As I watched him limping away towards his tied cottage where he'd lived by himself for the last ten years I couldn't understand how such a weak old bloke could have mastered such a big bad-tempered cow.

I worked with George all that holiday. It was a slack time of the year so we did all kinds of odd jobs, even making scarecrows and picking up buckets full of stones from the field at the top of the Mortar Pits. He never talked about the other men much but I knew he didn't like them; he did say Bill Morgan wasn't too bad but that he wasn't much of a foreman. He should make the young devils get off their backsides and do a bit more work.

In the last week before I went back to school we had to thresh a couple of wheat stacks. It took about six or seven men to thresh and me and George had to go and help. The threshing machine is pulled up to the side of the stack. Two men on the stack feed the sheaves to a man on the machine. He cuts the binder twine round the sheaf and drops the corn into the drum, a thing like they have now on the back of dust carts to grind the rubbish, only the drum on the threshing machine goes round six times as fast and makes a high-pitched noise as it swallows the sheaves. The corn comes out of the hole at the bottom of the machine, and is fed into sacks; each sack has eighteen stones of wheat in it so you need a strong bloke to carry the sacks to the barn. The straw comes out of a sort of chute on to an elevator and is carried up to where a stack is made of it. Old George was put to make the straw-stack himself.

I was put in the pult-hole. I still think being in the pult-hole on a threshing machine must be the worst job in the world. The pult is all the husks that remain when the grains of corn have been shelled out. This pult is shaken out of the belly of the threshing machine in a filthy shower. You have to dive under the machine, rake the pult on to a cloth and carry it to the crew-yard. On a calm day it's a filthy, back-breaking job. On a windy day it's murder. The whirling pult penetrates your clothes; you shake some of it out every five minutes but your body soon becomes one big itch. It takes three tubs of water at the end of a windy day in the pult-hole just to get the black out of your hair. But the worst thing is your eyes. Even if you could afford goggles in those days, they weren't much protection against the fine, black husks that found their way into the corners of your eyes. At the end of the day in the pult-hole you looked as if you'd been crying for about six weeks.

On the second day of threshing the wind was blowing almost gale-force and by the afternoon I was crying. I didn't let anybody notice though but at about three o'clock Master William turned up. He sat in his car for a bit looking out of the window. He then got out, pulled his trilby down, turned his collar up and fought his way through the wind to me.

'Can you manage boy?' he shouted above the noise of the wind and the threshing machine.

'No, I bloody can't. Could you?'

I thought Master William was a bit surprised when I said that. Perhaps he thought I was being cheeky or something. I didn't care anyway; I'd had enough of pult-holes to last me a lifetime.

Anyway Master William didn't say anything but went back to his car. He must have said something to Bill Morgan because he came and knocked me on the shoulder about ten minutes later.

'I'll do this for a bit, boy. You go and help George on the straw-stack.'

I didn't need asking twice. It was a relief to get away from the swirling filth and continuous whine of the drum.

When I got to the back of the straw-stack and began to climb the ladder I wasn't so sure. The stack was pretty high by now and it didn't look too safe to me. I crawled up the ladder and inched my way on to the stack. I stood in the middle, leaning on my fork. The wind was even stronger up here and I was sure the stack would blow over. Old George didn't seem to have any fear. He was taking huge forkfuls of straw from the top of the elevator, pushing it to the corners and sides of the stack and trampling it down with his old lace-up boots within a few inches of the edge of the stack. There was something wrong with George though. His face was red and his yellow teeth were set tightly together like a dead rat's in a trap.

'Blast the blasted awful wind,' said George, stamping towards me. 'What's the blasted sense in blasted well thresh-ing on a blasted day like to-blasted day. How the hell does that blasted burke William expect any bloke to manage up a blasted straw-stack by his blasted self in such a blasted rotten awful blasted wind. If he comes up here I'll stick this blasted fork in his blasted guts, I blasted well will. There's no blasted sense in it.'

I remember George 'blasting' away like this for about five minutes; he used a lot of other words as well that I'd never heard of, but they sounded pretty bad.

George shouted all this above the roar of the wind. As the afternoon wore on he got even madder. Twice he got to the top of the ladder to go down and wrap his fork handle round Master William's head. Each time he came back saying he would wait till knocking off time. I began to get worried for Master William. He wasn't such a bad bloke and I didn't think he quite deserved to be hung up like a fish with George's fork through his top lip. I lost count of the physical injuries Master William was to suffer. I wondered whether to go down and warn him but I was scared of the ladder. When the machine eventually stopped I crept slowly down the ladder. George came down after me two rungs at a time, carrying two forks in one hand. We got to the bottom and George limped quickly towards the barn. I followed him and just inside the door was Master William sitting on a bag of wheat, reading the *Daily Express*.

'Christ,' I thought, 'George will pin him to the sack like a rat.'

'Hello, George,' said Master William looking up. 'Are you all right up there?'

'Yes, thank you, Mr Wakefield,' said George without hesitation.

'Do you want any more help tomorrow or can you manage?'

'No, Mr Wakefield, I can manage all right, Mr Wakefield, thank you,' said George.

George picked up his basket containing the remains of his lunch and limped out of the barn.

'Are you all right up the straw-stack with George?' asked Master William.

'No, I ain't,' I said, 'I'd sooner go back to the pult-hole!'

The Twenty Pound Bike

'It's not fair!' I used to say that a lot when I was young. Later I found that there were so many things 'not fair' that there didn't seem much point in saying it. But I did notice that some things that were not fair had a way of putting themselves right. For instance, it wasn't fair that Skulker Wheat should never be out at cricket, or that Nob Hill should have a £20 bike while I didn't have a bike at all. It wasn't fair; but Skulker lost his front teeth because he wouldn't be out, and Nob Hill's bike got smashed up.

We used to play cricket on the grass area in front of Skulker Wheat's council house. It was quite a big area, but not big enough. When Skulker was batting you needed your best fielder in front of his house. He wasn't there to field the ball but to field Skulker when he ran to his Mam with the bat if we knocked his wickets down. If you didn't knock his wickets down he refused to be out. If he was caught it was always a 'bump' ball; he was never l.b.w. in his life. He was the worst sport I ever saw. But he owned the bat and this made a mockery of the saying: 'Cheats never prosper.' Skulker prospered by cheating for about two years. When we knocked over his wicket (which wasn't difficult) he would often run straight to his house with the bat, blaspheming dreadfully. Two minutes after he had gone through the door he would reappear with his Mam or Big Bonzo, his uncle.

'Give him another go,' his Mam would shout.

'He was out, Mrs Wheat; his wickets were knocked down.'

'Well, I've got my washing to do and the dinner to make.'

39

We didn't see the relevance of this argument but usually after about ten minutes negotiation Skulker would be back looking at us all in turn, suspiciously aggressive.

Well, one day Skulker's cheating led to his downfall. There was an old bloke in the village who often used to turn up to coach us. His name was Wally Dugdale and he had been a corporal in the RAF. He used to explain to us how to play forward and back with a straight bat. We didn't like him much but each of us had a secret hope that he might turn us into professional cricketers.

The sort of thing he told us to do didn't really work though. After a few weeks I realized that the things he taught us were all right if the pitch was flat; but the pitch in front of Skulker's house had so many potholes it looked like a minefield. Once the ball hit the pitch it could do four things: shoot off right or left, scuttle along the ground or jump up and hit you on the head. The one thing you could guarantee it wouldn't do was bounce a normal height and keep straight. We had adapted our own style to suit the pitch; dodging out of the way with our bodies and flailing at the ball with our arms at full stretch.

Wally was coaching us one day when a new kid who had come to stay with Mrs Turner for his holidays came out and sat on the grass.

We ignored him for a bit and then Fatty said, 'You want a game?'

'Yea, OK,' said the boy, standing up. He was quite a tall boy with long arms and a surly face. After a bit we gave him a bowl; he wasn't bad either. He stood near the wicket without taking a run but still bowled quite fast. He soon got Woolly out and a few minutes later he bowled one that scuttled along the ground and hit Skulker's wicket.

'Hold on, I wasn't ready,' said Skulker and threw the ball back.

'You're out, Billy,' said Wally Dugdale, who tried to be umpire, usually without much success.

'I wasn't looking; he bowled before I was ready.'

We didn't really expect to get Skulker out so quickly; you usually had to get him twice before serious negotiations began. So after a couple of minutes Skulker faced the bowling again. This new kid wasn't very pleased though; not that he said anything but he walked back about ten yards and took a run up to the wicket. The next thing we knew the ball was entering the ditch about seventy yards behind the wicket. We had a vague sight of it as it flashed by Skulker's head and past Jud Price, the wicket-keeper, but we only saw it properly as it slowed down to enter the ditch. It was easily the fastest ball we'd ever seen. Skulker obviously thought so too.

'It's about dinner-time,' he said and took off his pad; we had one old pad that the cricket club had lent us.

'It's only eleven o'clock. What's up with you?'

'Oh, is it?' said Skulker, looking surprised.

I think he would have gone home anyway if it hadn't been for Wally. I don't know whether he thought the honour of the village was at stake or something but he came up to Skulker and showed him how to play the 'forward defensive' stroke to fast bowlers.

'Put your left leg forward Billy and keep your body and head in line with the ball.'

It was about the silliest advice I've ever heard; but looking back over the years I think Wally gave it in good faith and Skulker had some hope that it might work. This new kid sat down about ten yards behind the wicket and waited till Wally had finished his coaching. I can still remember how the feeling of savage excitement in me changed to real concern when Skulker put his left leg and face forward and the ball hit him an awful blow in the mouth. He didn't seem to make much noise but when we got to him he was bleeding on his pad and on to the pitch; two of his teeth were on the grass but I couldn't see his mouth because he was holding it with both hands.

41

He was stitched at the doctor's in the afternoon and came out next morning looking subdued.

The incident wasn't only a lesson to Skulker; it affected all of us.

This new kid (he was a good friendly kid when we got to know him) stayed for five weeks. He never bowled fast again; he didn't need to. He somehow became the umpire. If one of us wasn't sure whether we were out we would ask his opinion, whether he was bowling or not. If he said, 'Yea, I think it was,' we would put down the bat immediately. Wally Dugdale didn't come much after that. He'd lost his influence over us and he knew it.

The incident was my first lesson in the exercise of power. In two seconds that kid had established more control over us than Wally Dugdale had done in six weeks; we were even sorry when he left.

Skulker was 'served right' by this boy; Nob Hill was 'served right' because my Uncle Dick was too mean to buy a new pig-rope.

I suppose you couldn't blame Nob for being a braggart; his mother was the most boastful woman I ever met. She was a little fat woman with a face like a barn owl's, her eyes blinking behind her black-rimmed glasses. Nob was a small version of her, only instead of glasses he had a red beret, like a French onion seller's.

One day when I was going up to Chunny James's to get the accumulator recharged for the wireless, this woman and her nasty son were standing on the corner outside the top pub. Parked against the kerb was a shining new green bike with all sorts of gadgets—four-speed gears, a dynamo, a huge green bell and even a water carrier stuck on the front. What annoyed me most about it was a little flag sticking up from the centre of the handlebars with 'Nigel' (Nob's name) written on it.

'Have you seen our Nig's new bike?' said Mrs Hill. 'It cost twenty pounds.'

I must admit I was very impressed but I didn't know what to say.

'Can I have a go on it?' I said eventually.

'No,' she said sharply, and then, trying to seem kind, 'not yet anyway; Nigel's not had many goes himself yet, have you dear?'

'No,' said Nob and mounting his bike, did a wobbly circle to show off.

'Careful, dear,' said Mrs Hill, as Nob put his brakes on too quickly and nearly fell off, 'that's enough for now.'

They had brought the bike to the busiest part of the village to catch people coming home from work or off buses so that they could brag about it.

When I got back up to the top of the village to meet my mates after tea, she was just pushing the bike home, leaving Nob behind to play. We didn't have much to do with Nob usually but I suppose he thought his £20 bike gave him a right to be with us. He didn't stay long though because after he'd said that his bike cost more than all ours put together (it was true), Jim Offord snatched his red beret and dipped it in Broddy Davies's water butt and hung it on Mrs Court's clothes line to dry, where Nob couldn't reach it. Nob went home roaring and Jim got worried because we said Nob's Mam would have the cops round. So he took the cap off the line and went to chuck it into Nob's garden.

About three weeks later me, my Dad and Uncle Dick went to kill Bertie, Nob's pig. Neither Nob nor his Mam or Dad (for some reason his Dad was a nice bloke) was in; the £20 bike was standing in the yard (it had legs that came down so you didn't have to lean it against walls). Every year Nob and his Mam went out when we came to kill his pig because they couldn't bear to hear it being killed. I didn't mind this because it's not a very nice thing to happen to something you like and as she'd only got Nob, I imagine she used to get quite fond of the pig. In fact I

43

wouldn't have been very surprised if we'd found Nob in the sty and Mrs Hill had gone out with Bertie. That was the arrangement I'd have made myself. What did used to annoy me though was how she acted when she came back.

'Have you really killed him?' she'd say.

'Yes, missus,' said Uncle Dick.

'Oh dear, I was rather hoping you wouldn't. Oh dear!'

And then she'd take out her handkerchief and start to cry. I thought about this as I looked at Bertie in his sty. How she'd come back shed a few tears and then eat him.

Well, I told you how to kill a pig before so I won't bore you again with the details. The only difference this time was that just as Uncle Dick was about to stab Bertie the rope I was holding broke and Bertie rushed squealing across the yard, put his head under the cross bar of the £20 bike and mangled it against the sty's opening as he belted for the security of his shelter. We all, even Uncle Dick himself, knew it was his fault because the rope was frayed and my Dad had been telling him for weeks to get a new one. But that didn't help us with the problem. We didn't know whether to kill Bertie first or try to straighten the bike. In the end we decided that killing Bertie was the easier job so we did that and an hour later my Dad was trying to bend the bike straight with his Wellington boots as levers.

'Do you think they'll notice, Dick?' said Dad as he stood the bike up and tried to push it without success.

'Course they will; you bloody fool,' said Dick and for once I was on his side. Sometimes my Dad's optimism was ludicrous.

'How much did you say it cost?' my Dad asked me.

'£20.'

'Christ, we can't afford that.'

They stood there scratching their heads for about five minutes.

'I know what we'll do,' said my Dad suddenly. 'You remember when our Frank hit that tree on his motor

44

bike? You know, when that tree was struck by lightning and fell across the road. Well, the insurance company wouldn't pay up would they? They said it was an "act of God". Wouldn't pay him a penny and his bike all twisted as a tin of spaghetti. Well, this is the same, isn't it? We'll say it's an "act of God".'

And that's what they did. Mrs Hill complained to the whole village, the police and probably the King too for all I know. But my Dad and my Uncle Dick stuck it out; they had to, they didn't have £20.

I thought it was an act of Uncle Dick, not God, and you couldn't get a bigger difference than that. Looking back now and remembering Nob and his odious Mam, I'm not so sure.

Baron Warthead

Are you scared of anything? I don't mean scared of a tiger or a policeman or anything like that; I mean scared of anything you've no reason to be scared of, like a spider or a grass-snake.

I'm scared of rats. When I was a boy, my Mam used to say to me, 'If you want some chips, go and get same tates out of the barn.' Suddenly I didn't fancy chips any more because going to the barn meant rats. If I couldn't avoid it, I used to creep up to the barn door and suddenly fling it open. Then I used to bash my bucket against the door and sing 'Come into the garden, Maud' at the top of my voice for about two minutes. Even the dimmest rats knew I was coming then and I hoped they'd be safely down their holes. Then I switched on the barn light and peered in. Sometimes there was a straggler running along the beams or up the steps to the loft at the end of the barn. I would scream a string of swear words at it, in a sort of desperate fear.

The sack of tates was usually at the far end and I would walk up to it quickly, swinging my bucket and whistling. A half-full sack of tates is just the place for a rat to be hiding and I swear my heart used to stop beating when I prodded the top with my foot. If one jumped out I would leap in the air and then run for the door; otherwise I'd quickly pour a few tates in the bucket and belt for the door like a madman.

Aren't you scared of rats? If you're not perhaps you haven't seen a wild one at close quarters. Look at its horrible sharp yellow teeth, its long bald tail and its splodgy fur. They're cunning too. I once saw one lying on its back holding a hen's egg in its paws and another pulling it along by its tail.

I once put my hand up on to a ledge to feel for a hen's egg and felt instead the fur of a rat. It was dead but it didn't look dead. They used to kill them with poison that made them bleed inside and die, so that they looked as if they'd just stopped running for a minute.

We once had a dog called Paddy, and it was bought for catching rats. The trouble was Paddy wouldn't go near a rat let alone catch one. My Dad was pretty mad about wasting his money and the next time a rat got itself caught in the corn-bin—the sides were too steep for it to get out—he put Paddy in the bin with it, shut the lid and rolled the bin up and down the barn. The rat bit Paddy and then Paddy killed it; after that he was a good ratter. The next time a rat got caught in the bin my Dad looked at me a bit funny so I scarpered; it was a big bin and I was quite small enough to fit in.

If you ever go threshing, wear leggings or tie up the bottom of your trousers with binder-twine. When the rats start running out of a stack they'll run anywhere and one day one ran straight up Sep Ramsden's trousers. He caught it just short of his whatsits and held on to it with both hands. Then he squeezed it slowly down his trouser leg and it emerged a bit dazed at the bottom. Then Sep stabbed it with his hayfork. I swear I would have died if it had happened to me.

If Woolly Lamb or Jud Price read this they wouldn't believe it. You see when they were around I was the fiercest rat-hunter of the lot. If I'd let on how scared I was of them, they'd have put one in my boot or something.

In the last war you could get a penny for every rat's tail you brought to my Uncle Dick who was the official rats' tail collector for the village. I took him hundreds—sometimes the same ones that we managed to nick back when he wasn't looking. We used to hunt them remorselessly with sticks, spades, hammers—anything that was handy. If I got one in the open I'd run after it—you can catch them easily because they only appear to run fast when you see one in a shed or small space—and kick it to death, screaming with rage at it. It was a sort of desperate rage though; none of my mates guessed I was terrified of them.

That's the mistake Baron Warthead made; he should never have let us know he was scared of cows. Baron Warthead was a clerk or something in the nearby town; he always went to work in a suit and, as you might have guessed, he had a wart the size of an egg-cup growing out of his head, round, pink and with ginger hairs on it. He was over fifty but he wasn't married—perhaps because of his wart—and he lived with his Mam in a cottage at the top end of the village. I suppose he was all right at clerking and that sort of thing but he wasn't too bright in other ways. For instance, one night he went down to the Labour Club and asked the old blokes in there the best way to grow celery. Walter Worthington and Freddie Thornton might not have been able to read very well but they could see someone like Baron Warthead coming a mile off.

Walter was just about to pot a blue in the middle pocket when Baron Warthead leaned over him: 'Excuse me, Walter, I wonder if you could help me in a little horticultural matter.'

He always spoke in a posh way; that's why we called him 'Baron'. Walter leant on his cue and looked Baron Warthead up and down.

'I'm extending my kitchen garden and would like advice on the growing of celery.'

'Celery,' said Walter, 'celery, Toby. That's a bit tricky.' (Baron Warthead's real name was Toby Waters).

'Do you think a four-foot or a six-foot trench, Freddie?' asked Walter.

'Six foot's best,' said Freddie, 'but I should think about five foot would be all right on Mr Waters' soil.'

'It depends how many bottles you're going to put in,' said Walter.

'Bottles?' asked Baron Warthead.

'Oh yes, for drainage; you need to line the trench with bottles; beer bottles is best but a few pop bottles won't hurt.'

'Then there's the treacle of course. Just spread about two big tins of treacle on top of the bottles,' said Walter.

'It siphons the goodness out of the water before it drains off through the bottles.'

Well, these old fools went on like this for a bit. Anybody with any sense would know they were taking the rise out of him right from the beginning. But Baron Warthead was pretty stupid in that way. I've noticed that about a lot of clever people; they're really stupid in some ways.

He did it all; deep trench, bottles, treacle, the lot. The funny thing was he did have a very good crop of celery.

His front lawn wasn't so good though because one day I was driving one or two cows from the Mortar Pits to the forty-acre. I was by myself which made it pretty hard, especially when folks didn't keep their gates shut. Baron Warthead's gate was shut all right but he had one of those dinky little walls with flowers in the top and this stupid Friesian just stepped over it and started frisking around the lawn. I tried to get behind it but it managed to sneak behind one of his big flower bushes. I went round the other side and belted its backside with a stick but all of a sudden there was this screaming voice from the up-stairs window.

'Get it out, get it out quick. I will not, will not have it. Get it out, out, out.'

Baron Warthead's face was white but I knew that it wasn't only rage; it was fear. Just like me with the rat. But how could anyone be afraid of a cow? Anyway, he tried

49

to sue my Dad for damage to his lawn and in the end my Dad gave him a quid to shut his mouth.

Bonfire night wasn't very exciting in our village; all the excitement was on Mischief Night, the night before. We used to meet in the village square about seven o'clock with our pockets full of bangers. We had no use for 'pretty flamers'; the only fireworks we were interested in were rockets, jumping-jacks and big bangers.

I knew it was going to be a good Mischief Night when all the usual things went off so well. We took Norris Hurton's iron gates off and hid them in the bushes. He'd got so used to this that one year he took them off himself before we came. We didn't quite know whether to put them back on again or not; we got the feeling he won that night. Then we set off a few bangers under a dustbin lid to see how high they would blow it. Next we chucked a banger into the Labour Club and had the satisfaction of being chased by Broddy Davies. We ran to the top of the village and arrived just in time to hear the Nottingham bus chugging up the hill.

'Watch me,' said Fatty and he did the daftest thing I'd seen anybody do for a long time. He lay down in the middle of the road pretending to be dead. It was lucky that he was near a street light because I think this helped the bus driver to see him. He braked hard and stopped. Up got Fatty and we all ran off laughing.

In the first two houses up Mill Road lived Nut Deakin and Nurse Pick. Nut was the blacksmith and pretty strong, but he wasn't a match for Nurse Pick when it came to pulling a front door open. That night was the only time I've seen the trick of tying two door-handles together work properly. We tied Nut's front door to Nurse Pick's with some pig rope I'd brought, and Woolly and Jud knocked on the two doors at the same time. We hid behind Dick Pearce's wall and watched. They really did try to open their doors at the same time.

Nut pulled up the short piece of slack in the rope first but Nurse Pick gave a grunt and tugged Nut's door shut. There was only enough slack rope for her to get her door half open, and she poked her head round to see what was the matter. Just then Nut gave his door an extra tug and shut Nurse Pick's door on her head. I've never heard anyone swear like Nurse Pick did then. I was really impressed by her foul language. It scared us a bit and we ran off in case she broke the rope and got out.

After that things were a bit dead. By nine o'clock we'd used up all our bangers and couldn't think of anything else to do. It was Woolly who suggested that we go and ride on Roany. Roany was an old cow of Wakefield's; the softest cow I'd ever seen. It would let three of you ride it at once and when it was fed up it just used to stand still and moo, refusing to move further whatever you did. But by the time we'd arrived at the paddock Jud had a better idea.

'Let's take her and put her through the Labour Club's door.'

'No, somebody would see us under the street lights, bound to,' I objected.

'If Baron Warthead was in there he'd have a fit,' said Fatty. We all knew Baron Warthead was scared of cows. They were such daft things to be scared of that it was a bit of a joke in the village.

'Pity we can't get her into his house,' said Woolly.

We all thought that would be a good joke but she would never get through his door, even if anyone was brave enough to open it.

'We could tie her to his door-handle and knock and run,' said Jud.

Now that was a good idea. We found some rope in Wakefield's stackyard and soon located Roany. She was the only cow who didn't get up and walk off when you approached her. We tied the rope round her neck and got her to her feet. She walked placidly with us along the pavement until we reached Baron Warthead's cottage. We led her cautiously up the path—we didn't want to spoil his grass again—and quietly tied her to the door-handle.

Then Woolly knocked loudly and we all ran and hid behind his big flower bush.

When Baron Warthead opened the door Roany looked at him and gave a moo—her face was about two feet from his. I expected him to shout and scream but he just stood there and didn't say anything. But then he sort of crumpled at the knees and fell on the floor, making a kind of low moaning noise.

We ran off as quickly as we could and all of us went straight home.

There was a terrible row about it next day. You see Baron Warthead had had a heart attack and they took him off to hospital. He got better all right but he was very quiet and sad-looking when he came out.

About six months later he went to live in the town where he worked; he was better off there anyway. We all got a good hiding from our Dads and they banned Mischief Night for the next year.

I was sorry about Baron Warthead but I couldn't help thinking he shouldn't have let us know he was scared of cows; I think he made a mistake there.

Wobble-Gob

There were one or two quite large orchards in our village and every season we used to go scrumping. We didn't steal the fruit on a large scale; I mean we didn't sell it or anything like that. We just took enough for ourselves to eat. Anyway, we knew from experience how easily you could get guts-ache from eating too many apples.

Sid Offord had a good orchard that backed up to an isolated field and we used to do quite a bit of scrumping of Sid's fruit every year. Three times I can remember he saw us and chased us down the lane. We ran fast but we weren't all that scared because we knew old Sid couldn't catch us. I don't think he tried very hard anyway; most of the people who owned fruit trees in the village would shout about fetching the police or telling our Dads if they caught us scrumping, but they never seemed to carry out any of their threats. I don't think they minded us old boys having a bit of fruit as long as we didn't take too much. We did our best not to get caught though, and we never were. Sid got within five yards of us one day and Woolly only just wriggled through the hedge in time; but that was the nearest anyone came to catching us.

One day though we wandered a bit off our usual track, down Church Hill and alongside the old railway line. It was scrumping season and when we came across a farm cottage with an orchard at the back, we peered through the hedge to see if there was any decent fruit on the trees. There was just what we fancied; some Victoria plums, about ripe, on a small tree hidden from the house windows by a large damson tree.

It was a tight squeeze through the little hole in the hawthorn hedge but we all managed it except Fatty Heathershaw, who was too fat and sat on a tree stump, waiting for us to come back. We didn't even have to climb the tree. The branches bent down and we soon filled our pockets, shirts and hands with large red plums. We struggled back through the hedge and were just walking away when a man's voice shouted, 'Hey, come back there, you young devils.'

We started to run, not all that fast because we were out of the orchard and confident we wouldn't be caught. We ran about fifty yards and then looked back. There was an oldish bloke coming after us but he was nearly a hundred yards away. But when we saw him we turned and ran as fast as we could, dropping plums from pockets and shirts in our panic. You see he'd only got one leg and was jumping along on a pair of crutches. We ran for about a mile before we were too breathless to continue.

'We'd better not go there again,' said Fatty, and we all agreed.

When I was in bed that night I thought about the incident for a long time. There didn't seem any sense in it; if he'd had two legs we wouldn't have been scared at all. Yet because he'd only one leg we were terrified; and what chance had he of catching us with only one leg? If he'd had two we'd have had far more reason to be scared.

We were scared of him just because of his one leg, and I think that's the reason we were always a bit scared of Wobble-Gob. Wobble was about two years older than the rest of us. He looked normal enough, a solidly built boy with black hair and a red face. But he was deaf and dumb. We used to go and call for him sometimes because he was quite good at football and cricket. He lived down the council houses next to Skulker Wheat.

The first time we went to call I made a mistake. Woolly knocked at the door and Wobble's mother opened it.

'Is your Wobble in?' I asked.

She was a sharp-faced woman and she gave me a nasty look.

'If you mean Billy I'll go and see,' she answered eventually.

When she went to look for him Woolly said to me, 'You stupid ass; she doesn't like you to call him Wobble.'

I felt a bit crushed but I didn't really understand what I'd done wrong. Everybody called him Wobble-Gob, and he didn't seem to mind.

When Wobble appeared he said, 'Ug, ug,' and off we went. All Wobble ever said was 'Ug, ug' in an excited, squeaky way. When he was playing football he said it all the time he had the ball but in a fierce way. I used to think he was fantastic at football, but after the incident with the one-legged man I thought about Wobble a bit more carefully. If he got the ball at football he would rush about shouting, 'Ug ug,' and he seemed to be able to get past everybody. I don't think it was skill though; I think we were all too scared to tackle him hard, what with him 'Ug, ugging' and not being able to shout if he was fouled or anything.

At cricket he used to hold the bat right at the end of the handle so that he could get a good swing at the ball. Every ball he swung at in a great flailing arc, the momentum turning his body right round to bring his bat back into the crease so he couldn't be stumped. If he hit one properly it used to go miles. He was often 'six, out and fetch the ball back' over Acton's wall. He missed far more than he hit though. If you could avoid his line of swaft and weren't put off by the tremendous 'Ug' he made just as you were about to bowl, you could usually get him out in his first over.

There was a posh woman living in a big red house on the outskirts of our village. She was called Mrs Bradbury and her husband was a Lieutenant-Colonel; he was about the nastiest person I've ever met. Once, a poor bloke living in a cottage rented from him had a quarrel with his wife. The noise was so bad that quite a crowd gathered. The woman was sitting outside the house on the pavement and the bloke was arguing with her, trying to make her go back into the house. After a few minutes this big Lieutenant-Colonel bloke came pushing his way through the crowd. He walked up to the poor bloke, got hold of him by his shirt collar, hit him on the jaw with his other fist and knocked him out. Then he strode off back without saying a word; that was the sort of bloke this Lieutenant-Colonel was.

His missus wasn't too bad though. She used to try to organize us kids into a club; it was all right till she caught us playing football with the ping-pong ball and then she cancelled the club.

Once she told us she was taking us to the White City in London on a bus. I was really excited about this. I was quite interested in athletics and used to listen to commentaries on races from the White City on Wally Dugdale's wireless. This Mrs Bradbury had a big son called Rodney; he talked in a very posh voice but he wasn't too bad in a smarmy sort of way. I was surprised on the bus when he started throwing paper balls and orange peel about. We had quite a good fight for a bit until Wobble hit this Rodney in the gob with an apple core. Rodney said, 'Let's knock it off now, chaps. We're in the outskirts of the city.'

I didn't see what difference that made but we 'knocked it off' all the same; after all his Mam was paying for us.

What a disappointment that outing was. Instead of athletics it was weedy-looking horses jumping over little fences. There were posh blokes in top hats riding them and sticking their wide backsides in the air every time they jumped the fences. And to cap it all this commentator bloke kept droning on in a posh, bored voice about 'faults' and 'refusals' and things. I've never been so disgusted in my life. That was the last time I was going on an outing with Rodney Bradbury and his Mam.

When she sent a note round to our Mams saying she'd organized a snowball fight though, we had to go; they always made us go to anything that she did. We didn't know what to expect; we didn't go in for snowball fights ourselves. You couldn't really hurt each other with snowballs unless you held them for a long time in your hands until they turned to ice but this slowed the whole thing down and we never saw much point in it in the first place. Skulker Wheat used to put bricks inside the snowballs before he chucked them but we stopped him doing that; he could have really hurt somebody.

Anyway, when we got to Bradbury's paddock it was just growing dark. The snow had been around for nearly a week and it was quite thick. Mrs Bradbury and Rodney had made two great piles of snow about two hundred yards apart. There were a few trees and bushes in between; on top of each pile of snow was a lantern and a flag. She explained that we could have two teams, and each team had to try to capture the other team's flag and bring it back to its own pile. We weren't to fight with fists, just snowballs.

It sounded all right so we picked up sides. Rodney Bradbury was captain of one side and Fatty Heathershaw of the other. Mrs Bradbury said the two teams were Spartans and Paladins. I didn't know what she was on about but the sides were clear enough. Fatty picked Wobble-Gob first and Rodney picked me. I'd sooner have been on Wobble's side but I wasn't too worried because at least Skulker was on my side; there was no telling what Skulker would do in the dark.

It was a good snowball fight. Nobody fouled by fighting with fists. Rodney Bradbury threw snowballs like a madman and when one of their side went home for his supper we started to drive them back to their flag. It was getting really dark now but you could still see the flags because of the lanterns. In the end we got their side pinned down by a barrage of snowballs behind the last tree before their flag. I sneaked round the bush that was just to the right of the tree and made a quick rush to their flag. Nobody was there and I reached out to grab it.

'Ug, ug,' said Wobble, leaping from where they'd posted him behind the wall of snow.

The next thing I knew there was Mrs Bradbury bending over me, asking if I was all right.

'Yes,' I said, standing up quickly. 'I just fell over and hit my head on a stone.' I said it several times, hoping they would believe me, even though there wasn't a stone in sight. I wasn't going to tell them that I'd passed out in fear at the sudden appearance of Wobble in the light of their lantern.

If only he'd said something like, 'I'll kill you,' or 'I'll smash your face in,' I'd have been all right though. It was the 'Ug, ug' that scared me.

About five years later I saw Wobble-Gob again. He'd left school and was working on a building site in town. 'Ug, ug,' he said and waved in a friendly way. I waved back. What struck me about him was that he looked so normal carrying bricks up a ladder. Of course he was normal, like the one-legged bloke. In fact there wasn't a friendlier more pleasant lad than Wobble in the village.

He did used to scare me though, when I was little.

Dumpy Cackitt

The main street of our village was about two hundred yards long and on a steep slope. There was a pub at each end and just before you came to the top pub, The Green Duck, there was the only gap in the old crumbling red-brick houses which made an otherwise solid wall between the two pubs. It wasn't a big gap, about three yards, but as you passed through it you suddenly found yourself in a rectangular block of much-trampled grass. At each corner of the grass stood a narrow-windowed, squat and thatch-roofed house: this was Dandelion Mews and in the smallest and dingiest of the four houses lived Dumpy Cackitt and his Dad, Mouthy.

When I was eight, my Mam had scarlet fever and went into what they called an isolation hospital, but it was really a big, rusty corrugated shed with a snappy old woman called Nurse Pick in charge. My Mam was in isolation for six weeks and during that time I had my dinner or tea in just about every house in the village. One day I went to Mouthy's and this was the first time I'd met either Mouthy or Dumpy at close quarters. Mouthy was small, thin and always wore a greasy cheese-cutter cap; he had two whole rows of big teeth the wrong side of his lips. They'd gone yellow as well, from too much exposure, I suppose. Dumpy was thin, like Mouthy, but though he was only sixteen he was well over six feet, a bean-pole of a boy with a sharp ferret-face.

I didn't eat much tea that day but I found out two interesting things; the first was that Mouthy's teeth were retractable. We had toast and jam and Mouthy ate his outside his mouth. The damp toast and the red jam went round and round in Mouthy's yellow choppers until they were wet enough and properly mixed. Then Mouthy made a sudden gulping noise and toast and jam and teeth all disappeared for about two seconds before his teeth would pop out again. I wasn't quite sure whether the trick was done by Mouthy's teeth going back or his mouth going forward. Anyway, I didn't eat much of my toast and jam. To be honest, Mouthy put me off a bit.

The other thing I found out was what a good footballer Dumpy was; he talked about his dribbling, heading, swerving and trapping skill for the whole of my visit; and when he wasn't mixing his tea Mouthy would put in a word of agreement.

'Yus, that's right, it's true that, yus it's true all right that is, yus.'

Mouthy made this speech about six times but with double emphasis when Dumpy was describing his special skill; his ability to 'beat 'em on the long run'. No matter, it seemed, how dedicated, skilful and fierce the opponent, Dumpy could always 'beat him on the long run'.

I didn't quite understand what he meant by this but I didn't want to ask and show my ignorance. But I did remember how good Dumpy was because in the next school holiday when we were getting our team organized to go and play Marfield—the nearest village to ours—I suggested to Woolly, who was our captain, that as we'd only got six players we should go and call for Dumpy and ask him to play for us.

'But he's too big,' said Woolly.

'He's brilliant though.'

'Yea, maybe he is, but he's ... well I bet he's about twenty.'

'No, he's sixteen—he's just tall for his age. Anyway Marfield never said anything about how old you have to be. He lives in the village, don't he?'

Eventually the six of us—I was eight, and Woolly was the oldest of us, having just had his ninth birthday—went round on our bikes to call for Dumpy. Mouthy answered the door.

'Please, Mr Cackitt, is your Albert in?' (Dumpy's real name was Albert but people called him Dumpy because he was so long and thin.)

'Yus,' said Mouthy, 'yus, he's in all right, yus, he's in, he is, yus.'

Fortunately Dumpy loomed up behind Mouthy otherwise Mouthy might have gone on 'yussing' so long, we'd have been late for the match. We had no trouble in persuading Dumpy to play.

'Yus, right boy, I'll get my boots,' was all he said and we were very grateful—that he had real football boots of course was a confirmation of his skill.

The Marfields were decidedly hostile. It was only when we had parked our bikes, set up our goals (Woolly's coat was one goalpost and Jud's the other) and were 'shooting-in' that they realized Dumpy was going to play.

'Who's he then?'

Two of them had wandered down our end to check the width of our goals—six normal paces of an 'average-sized' boy.

'Who's he then?' one of them repeated more loudly, because we had pretended not to hear first time.

'It's Dumpy.'

'He's not playing?'

'Course he is, what's wrong with him?'

'What's wrong with him! He's ... he's a bloke, isn't he?'

'Don't be stupid. He's only twelve!'

'Twelve, twelve?' The fat face of the Marfield captain went red, outraged by the enormity of our lie.

It took twenty minutes of negotiation before it was agreed that we could have Dumpy in our team. He took little part in the argument beyond admitting with a sly

61

grin that he was 'nearly thirteen'. But as the Marfields had nine men and we only had seven, including Dumpy, they eventually agreed to start. Dumpy had spent the twenty minutes of negotiation doing some impressive tricks with the ball. I noticed, though, that when he was practising dribbling he did seem to kick the ball rather a long way ahead each time, but I supposed he was so fast that he caught up with it just as quickly as someone who dribbled normally.

We had no doubt of his skill and knew we were going to hammer Marfield. Dumpy turned out to be brilliant. Admittedly he didn't get past anybody or make much progress towards the Marfield's goal but at 'beating 'em on the long run' he was sensational. Marfield's pitch was in the middle of a thirty-acre field and in those days we didn't have any touchlines. The boundaries were the distant hedges; the only rule was that if you took the ball beyond the opponent's goal they had to let you bring it back into play before tackling you.

The first time Dumpy got the ball he set off sideways in the direction of the distant hedge. For the first fifty yards or so he was harassed by about five Marfields, snapping at his spindly legs and shouting, 'Loony, Lanky, Larry.' He looked like a latter-day Gulliver as he gradually shook off his pigmy opponents until he had outdistanced them all. The Marfields arranged themselves in front of their goal and waited for him to return. He sat on the ball in the far distance for about two minutes. We were all excited as he began his run-in; the Marfields looked scared but as he got about twenty yards from the goal one of them luckily tackled him, took the ball and they scored.

We were still pretty confident though and when Woolly got the ball he passed it to Dumpy immediately. Off set Dumpy on his long circling run. This time the Marfields didn't chase him so far—they knew when they were beaten. When Dumpy brought the ball back he looked in pretty bad shape; he was gasping and sagging a bit at the knees. He toe-ended the ball to Jud.

'Here you are boy, I've done enough; some of you have a go.'

Dumpy beat the Marfields on the run at least twenty times that afternoon. Unfortunately the rest of us played badly; we usually beat the Marfields but at half-time they were winning 9–0.

Soon after half-time Dumpy had an accident. There was a farm cottage in the far corner of the field and the old woman who lived there used to hang her washing in the field. She hadn't any washing out today but she'd left the line up. Dumpy set off on one of his long runs and, perhaps refreshed by the bottle of pop they'd had at half-time, the Marfields pursued Dumpy further than usual. One was particularly persistent but Dumpy kicked the ball about thirty yards ahead and sprinted after it to shake him off. Suddenly Dumpy's head stopped and his legs kept going. I thought he was taking off; his legs climbed higher and his head remained stuck on the clothes line. He dropped to the ground and lay still. We all gathered round him. There was a bright red mark on his neck and his eyes were glazed.

'Are you all right, Dumpy?'

'Yus,' Dumpy said, with a croaky voice.

He didn't play again until a few minutes from the end. We scored four goals while he was having a rest and when he came back he scored himself. Well, we thought he scored but the Marfields said that they'd stopped playing. One of them had picked up his goalpost jacket and two more were taking their boots off, but I'm sure the ball would have been in if the goalpost was there. Anyway we lost 13–5 and as we set off home on our bikes the Marfields jeered about Loony Larry and one threw his pop-bottle at Dumpy's bike. We all thought we would have won if Dumpy hadn't had his accident; he agreed.

'Trouble is,' he said, 'you can't do it all on your own;

you need somebody to help you.' We felt ashamed.

We didn't see Dumpy again for about six months, but one night we were riding our bikes in circles, as usual, just outside the top pub when he joined us.

There was a girl who lived next door to Dumpy in Dandelion Mews called Alice Weaver and this bald-headed bloke called Rupert used to come from town on the Silver Queen bus and stand kissing and mauling her under the lamp-post outside Dandelion Mews. He started doing it about ten minutes after Dumpy had joined us. We all hated Rupert because he was bald and didn't live in the village, but we were all scared of him; Woolly reckoned that his Dad had told him Rupert was thirty.

Anyway this night we started to edge up to Rupert and this Alice Weaver to see if we could see what they were doing; as usual though as soon as we got within twenty yards Rupert told us to 'get lost' and we did. But when we got back to our area Dumpy shouted out at Rupert.

'Rupert, the rat, the snipe-nosed rat bag from Rotterdam.' I didn't know what it meant but it must have been pretty bad because Rupert set off after Dumpy before his words had died away. I suppose Dumpy thought he could 'beat him on the long run'; but he didn't get a chance because Rupert the rat had caught him before he'd gone twenty yards. The fight lasted about ten minutes and I had to admit that Rupert seemed to be giving Dumpy a good hiding; in the end Rupert got Dumpy on his knees and was pulling his hair with his left hand and throttling him with his right. Dumpy turned his head slowly and his nose was all bloody. He looked up at Rupert and said, 'Have you had enough, boy? Have you had enough?'

Rupert laughed and let Dumpy go. When Rupert was out of sight Dumpy said, 'That showed him; he won't come back here again in a hurry.'

As I went home that night, I began to have my first doubts about Dumpy.

Dick

'Watch out behind you, mister.'

Almost every kid has shouted something like this when the 'baddy' is creeping up on the 'goody' at the pictures. Nearly all of us used to shout out and join in with the film when I used to go to the Grenadiers on Saturday mornings in the local town. I used to become very involved with the film—usually a cowboy—and when at the end Uncle Harry put the lights on we paused and looked at each other before catching the bus.

'Wasn't bad,' someone would say.

'No, not too bad.'

'It was OK, wasn't it?'

Not bad—it was marvellous! Especially the bit where the cavalry came charging over the hill to rescue the bloke who was trussed up, hanging upside down over a blazing fire, about to be fried by dancing Indians.

But no matter how much we hated the 'baddy' and got excited by his diabolical schemes, we never rushed forward to knock him over. We always knew, even at that young age, it wasn't that real.

Not like these Indian hillsmen a mate of mine told me about when I was much older. Apparently in some parts of India, films are shown in the open air. A van pulls up in a village, two blokes set up a primitive screen and they collect money in a tin from people who want to stand around and watch. Well, this Indian friend said that when the 'baddy' came on, half the audience used to pull out their guns and 'shoot' him. The travelling film blokes used to spend half their time repairing holes in the screen that the previous night's audience had made.

My gran used to annoy me when she came round to see the telly. She wouldn't shut up and let you watch in peace. She kept up a running commentary on the action. The first thing she'd do when she arrived was sit herself in the best chair in the front room and take her pipe from the pocket of her old green cardigan. She used to smoke Digger Flake; black greasy-looking stuff like a lot of rats' tails in a tin. She'd take out a rat's tail and rub it between her horny wrinkled hands. When it was shredded enough she'd stuff it in the big black bowl of her pipe and light up. She was soon enveloped in a cloud of smoke, which was not, unfortunately too thick for her to see the telly.

'Ooh, look at him, the old devil,' she would growl when the 'baddy' came.

'Ooh, what's he doing now? Ooh, would you believe it? I'd like to strangle him. Ooh, the crafty old devil.' And so it went on. She enjoyed the films all right; we didn't much when she was there.

But I don't think any of us, me as a kid, my gran, even the Indian hillsmen ever thought what was happening in front of us was real. None of us thought the heroine was a real woman being strangled before our very eyes. If we had done, I suppose we should have tried to stop it. I know the hillsmen did try, but I think even they knew their bullets weren't doing the 'baddy' any harm.

Now Dick Dobson couldn't distinguish between real and make-believe. When I was about eight only Dick and Mike Dugdale were the same age as me in my village. So the three of us used to play together. Unfortunately Dick was very thick. One incident some years later will show how thick old Dick was. During the last war there was this slogan 'Dig for Victory'. They were always saying it on the wireless, trying to make people keep allotments and get farmers to plough up grassland and grow more crops.

One day when Silas Rudkin, the headmaster, was taking

66

us for gardening (Rural Science they call it now) he called us all together, leant on his hoe and said, 'Well, boys, why are we digging the soil?'

He'd told us already. It was something to do with letting air in, and worms came into it as well; I've forgotten the details. Nobody answered him at first and this annoyed him, especially as he'd been telling us all about it the week before. He repeated the question, 'Why do we dig?' and Dick put his hand up, a most unusual occurrence.

'Yes, Dobson.'

'Victory, sir.'

Silas Rudkin lifted up the hoe he was leaning on and hit Dick on the head with it. He hit him quite hard too, and Dick fell down in a stunned heap, which was very unfair, because Dick really thought he'd got the answer.

Anyway you can see that if Dick was that thick at twelve or thirteen, he was even less bright when he was eight. But Dugdale and I still played with him—there wasn't much choice. Dugdale and I were quite imaginative kids but even we found it difficult to imagine the two of us were a whole tribe of Indians. With three it was easier. Dugdale and I could be the chiefs and we had Dick as a brave—there wasn't much point in our being chiefs if there was no one to order about.

I remember clearly the first time I found that Dick had difficulty in distinguishing what was real and what was imaginary. It was one day when we were attacking the tribe called Tom Waltham. Old Tom had a smallholding of about fifty acres and it used to take him about a fortnight to side hoe and single his mangolds. There he was every day, a solitary figure bent over his hoe, with no cover except a thin hawthorn hedge to protect him from a whole tribe of Indians. Dugdale, Dick and I filled him so full of imaginary arrows in the first two days that there wasn't the smallest piece of flesh left to aim at. On the third day we became a bit bored by his lack of retaliation—there he was, hoeing away, completely unaware that he had been killed a hundred and fifty times. So we raided his ammunition dump—his lunch box and flask of tea left near the gate under the hedge. Dugdale and I ran through the ammunition dump first—I 'shot' the flask and Dugdale kicked his lunch box, taking care to miss it. After us came the 'brave' who jumped on his flask, smashed it to smithereens and emptied his sandwiches in the hedge.

'What did you do that for?' I asked, scared and angry.

I looked at Dick's face, round and vacant. His narrow forehead underneath his greasy flat black hair started to frown. I knew from the look of him he didn't even understand the question. If Tom Waltham was the enemy why didn't we get him? Dugdale and I ran away and Dick lumbered behind us, puzzled and fed up. We didn't go near Tom Waltham's field for a long time.

There were other signs during the next few months that Dick was a dangerous companion. He put a stone from his catapult through Horace Pulfrey's window when he was supposed to miss, and when we captured a pride of dangerous marauding lions—Mrs Bradbury's chickens—Dick stamped on one's head and killed it. We were lucky to get away with the window and the dead chicken, but Dugdale and I decided that we'd better not bother with Dick any more. But he kept coming to call for us and we hadn't the heart to turn him away—we were a bit scared of him as well.

The climax came one afternoon when Dugdale went to get his hair cut. We had a den at the bottom of Arthur Jansen's long garden. It was the best den we ever had; actually it had been Arthur's toilet until six months before when he had a proper flush one installed in his house. It was one of those two-seater earth toilets that had gone out of fashion even then. It was a red-brick structure about nine feet square. You opened the green door and the only furnishing was on the far wall, a sort of bench about two

feet high; there were two holes side by side in the bench—
and that was the complete toilet. Of course it was deeply
dug out below the two holes, otherwise the smell would
have suffocated old Arthur and his family.

It didn't smell much now though, and was a perfect
den, screened from Arthur's house by an enormous damson
tree. It really was the biggest and most flourishing tree
I've ever seen, a tribute, I suppose, to Arthur's rich
living.

Dugdale, Dick and myself used to use this toilet as a
den quite a lot. We even had candles in bottles on the
bench so that we could go and sit there at night. The one
who arrived first would 'lock' the door by slipping a piece
of wood under the latch and when the next one of us came
he couldn't get in unless he used the password—'chicken-
run'. I can't remember how we chose 'chicken-run' as the
password.

Well, on the morning of the day I was telling you about,
we had been in the den about an hour planning the murder
of Mrs Bradbury's posh son, Rodney, who had come home
from his boarding school for the holidays. We knew he had
a gun; we'd seen him shooting pigeons with it so we had to
plan our moves very carefully to avoid being shot. You can
imagine my annoyance when, having worked out a detailed
plan to murder Rodney after dinner, Dugdale suddenly remembered that he had to go and have his hair cut instead.
He saw that I was mad so he said he'd hurry back on the
quarter-to-four bus so that we could begin the murder
at four.

Dick and I were in the den by three. We waited until a
quarter past four but Dugdale didn't appear. I was even
more annoyed than in the morning, so I explained to Dick
that Dugdale was a traitor now and was probably plotting
with Rodney Bradbury to murder us. We must never let
him in the den again. Dick seemed to understand all right
and helped me to purify the den of the lingering presence

of the traitor, Dugdale. We did this by dropping his belongings, a candle and a box of marbles, down one of the toilet holes. There were two faint plops several seconds after we dropped them; it must have been miles deep, a discovery which increased my anger because it showed what a perfect choice we had made for the disposal of Rodney Bradbury's body—when we had cut him into small enough pieces to go down the holes.

The next thing we did was change the password. Dick couldn't think of any and I could think of too many. Eventually we decided on 'double-barrel' which I probably thought of as it was the type of gun Rodney Bradbury was liable to shoot us with. While Dick was repeating 'double-barrel' to make sure he could remember it, there was a knock at the door and somebody started trying to lift up the latch. I looked through the keyhole, saw Dugdale's tatty red shirt and shouted, 'Password?' Dugdale shouted, 'chicken-run,' and tried the latch again, confidently expecting the piece of wood to have been removed. When he found he still couldn't get in he shouted the old password even louder and kicked at the door.

'Wrong,' I shouted back. I turned to Dick and told him, 'Prepare to repel traitors.'

We picked up our clubs (thatchpegs stolen from Tommy Waltham) and waited behind the door.

It's pretty obvious what happened. You may say I should have known better even at that age. Perhaps I should, but I think I'd forgotten how dangerous Dick was in the excitement. Once Dugdale got in I was prepared to let him stay and work on the proposed murder plan.

Dugdale charged at the door with his shoulder and after about six goes he smashed the latch. As he came tumbling in Dick hit him a fearful blow in the face with his thatchpeg. A thatchpeg is quite heavy and Dugdale was making the effect worse by running into the blow. There was Dugdale, blood gushing from mouth, nose and left eye, and would you believe it, Dick was about to hit him again.

'Stop it,' I shouted, really frightened. 'What did you do that for?'

As soon as I said the words I remembered how familiar they were, how often I'd said them to Dick over the last few months. I looked at Dick as he dropped his thatchpeg. He stared at me, puzzled. He couldn't understand how I could go on about Dugdale's treachery and the necessity to stop him entering and then blame him when he had stopped him so effectively. I knew that it wasn't any good explaining but I also knew it had to be the last time I played with Dick.

It also might be the last time I played with Dugdale; he still wasn't moving and the blood was continuing to seep out of him. Dick helped me carry him outside the toilet and lay him under the damson tree. I looked at him carefully for signs of movement; I knew if I went to fetch his Dad or any adult that would be the end of the den. But it had to be done; I couldn't let him die under a damson tree.

'Please, Mr Jansen, will you come and look at Mike Dugdale? I think he's hurt himself.'

Well, it all had to come out. Poor old Dugdale had fifteen stitches in his head and was off badly for a whole week. Me and Dick got terrible hidings for it and although Dick was the one who actually hit Dugdale, I think I deserved my belting more than Dick.

A few years later, to add to his troubles, Dick had his foot cut off by a binder. You don't see many binders about nowadays, combine-harvesters have taken their place.

They used to look and sound good; the six-foot serrated-edged knife rattling backwards and forwards mowing down the corn; the great wooden slats called sails revolving as they pushed the corn on to the knives; the corn finally being spewed out in neatly tied bundles, after travelling up the canvases to the knotting machine.

71

Binders certainly looked good, but they could be dangerous especially to boys in pursuit of rabbits that were likely to dodge out of the corn just in front of the binder.

'Stand back, get out of the way, watch the knife.' These would be continuous warnings to us from the man on the binder.

Well, one day poor old Dick wasn't quick enough and his foot was so badly cut around the ankle that it had to be amputated. We didn't need any warnings after that!

Dick never got a job as far as I can remember—until he became park superintendent. In the middle of our village was a scrubby half-acre of land called the park. It wasn't much of a park, a couple of benches given 'In loving memory of Mollie Seaton'—whoever she was—a pond covered in slimy green weed, a few ducks, a couple of moorhens and three kids' swings. It didn't need a superintendent, of course, but Dick sat on one of the benches most of his time and in the end somebody gave him a peaked blue cap with 'Superintendent' written on it. Dick was real proud of his hat and instead of sitting on the bench he used to hobble about his park, keeping an eye on the swings and the pond. Then he put up a notice saying DON'T FEED THE DUCKS. Nobody did anyway so it didn't matter. There was once a bit of trouble when he hit a little lad over the head with his walking stick for standing on a swing. But he wasn't too hurt and nobody minded much because it was Dick. After that if there was any misbehaviour in his park, Dick was told he should report it at the Post Office on his way home. Mrs Auden, the postmistress, always said that she'd contact 'the authorities' for him and Dick seemed quite happy. It didn't seem to worry him that 'the authorities' never came round to check on his work, nor did he bother that his wages were paid by the sickness benefit people rather than the 'Park Authorities.'

It was odd that after all I've told you about Dick, the

job he got was an imaginary one. It was real enough to Dick though and as far as I know he still hobbles happily around his park 'superintending' his ducks and swings.

The Football Pools Winner

Some people get mad quicker than others. I know that sounds obvious but it's always surprised me how easy it is to turn some people into raging maniacs. All you had to do with Skulker Wheat, for instance, was to look straight at him and count. By the time you'd reached twenty, he would be taking a kick at you with his old black lace-up boots, or looking round for a stone big enough to knock your head off. You could get him mad even quicker by pretending you'd been counting for some time under your breath and had just started to do it out loud.

'A hundred and sixty, a hundred and sixty-one ...' that was usually enough to start him up on a good day. Then you'd run out of the way of his flying boots and bricks and, at a safe distance, pretend to squint towards him and shout, 'Five thousand and seventy four,' or something like that: you see he thought you were counting the freckles on his face. Not that there was anything wrong with his freckles, except that he looked as if he had jumped in a bowl of gravy. The trouble was, he thought we were laughing at him and that was enough to set him off like a fourpenny banger.

Another kid who was easily turned into a raving maniac was Fred Christian. He was a big red-faced farmer's lad and when we were in Junior School he had to sit next to a girl called Joyce. This Joyce was a bit advanced for her nine years and took a fancy to Fred. She used to write him notes saying she loved him and all that, and poor old Fred used to go as red as a Nottingham bus and shuffle his feet. He daren't get mad with this Joyce, but if the rest

74

of us lads said anything Fred was up swearing and pelting like a bad 'un. We used to sing hymns every morning in school and quite often we sang this hymn which went 'Rejoice, rejoice, Emmanuel' or something like that.

One day when we were playing football at break there was an argument about whether Fred had fouled this little lad Davies and whether it should be a penalty. Fred got his way, because he was bigger, but suddenly Davies started singing, 'Rejoice, rejoice, Emmanuel,' and putting a strong emphasis on the 'joice' part. It was enough for Fred. He went for poor little Davies like a lunatic and we had to pull him off. After that we only had to hum the tune and Fred would start pelting or fighting.

Fred and Skulker were very quick to lose their tempers but my Dad boiled much more slowly. He only got mad about twice a year and the first time he really lost his head taught me the importance of football pools.

Every Saturday about five he would be hunting through drawers, endlessly turning out the same ones, feeling three or four times in the pockets of his multitude of old coats. He could never find his copy coupon in time for the results on the wireless, but he usually had it ready for the arrival of the *Football Post*. He would sit with the coupon and I would read out the results.

'Tottenham?' he would say, bending over the table—he never sat down when checking.

'2–1.'

'Damn!' There was a pause as he started sucking his pencil to make it write.

'Birmingham?'

'1–0.'

'Oh, Christ! I've had it now.' Another interval while he bit pieces of wood from the pencil to expose enough lead to write with.

'Fulham?'

'0–1.'

'Oh, blast! It's no use going on.'

'Shall I stop then?'

'No, what about Brighton?'

'Draw, 1–1.' He grunted in satisfaction and pencilled it in. The most he ever won though was three shillings, when almost every team in the Football League drew.

One Saturday though, he wouldn't take me to a whist drive in the village. I wanted to go quite badly and nobody else would go with me. I was mad with disappointment and when he started reading his teams out on Saturday night I had a sudden idea to annoy him. The first three he read out I said were draws, although they were all home wins. He got excited, bit his pencil end off, snatched a fag and started puffing like a steam train. When he read out the next one I started to get a bit panicky.

'Grimsby?' he said, quietly but intently.

'Draw, 7–7,' I said, going through with my plan but trying to make it clear by the preposterous score that I was joking.

It was no good though; his ears were only tuned to the word 'draw' and if I had said, 'Draw, 28–28,' he wouldn't have noticed.

I can't remember clearly what happened after he'd found out. I know I spent some time hiding in the coalhole, some time collecting my belongings which had been thrown in the crew-yard, and that at one stage I set off to drown myself in the canal. The canal was three miles away so I never quite got round to committing suicide but I know it was three days before relations were nearly back to normal.

Anyway, the incident taught me that football pools were not something to joke about so I was as awed as the rest of the village when we heard that Billy Barstow had had a big win on the treble chance. Billy was a big fat-faced bloke about forty who worked for the Co-op delivering milk. He lived by himself in a small cottage at the top end of the village. He was a cheery enough bloke, a bit pot-bellied from too many evenings spent in the White Hart, but quite normal and friendly. His only hobby apart from drinking was following the hounds—on foot, of course, because Billy wasn't rich enough to have a horse or a car.

Now things were different. The first thing Billy did was buy a great big bay hunter called Daisy and he joined the Caythorpe Hunt. I think this was the start of Billy's un-doing. In a ratcatcher hat, a pair of Wellingtons and carry-ing a beet-pulp bag under his arm in case it rained, Billy looked all right. Sitting on Daisy, tarted up in his red jacket, black hat and carrying a crop, he looked awful. He didn't seem to fit in with the hunting lot at all. I don't know why they let him in: probably for his money; per-haps he paid extra. But he hadn't got the right sort of face. Most of the Caythorpe Hunt had faces like their horses and Billy's round moon of a face looked more suitable for chewing a straw than shouting 'tally-ho'. But the worst thing was, he couldn't ride.

I only saw him once at a Hunt meeting—his last—but he gave us old boys a real laugh.

'Hey up, Bill,' we shouted at him when he turned up in his full gear outside the top pub on the first Boxing Day after he'd won his fortune. He pretended we hadn't spoken; I don't think he wanted his new friends to see him talking to a gang of ragged kids on bikes—we always followed the hunt on bikes.

'Where's your horn, Bill?' shouted Skulker.

Bill turned away and downed his stirrup-cup in one— it was about the only thing he did right, the drinking part, although I think he'd have preferred a pint of bitter to whatever they were all drinking out of their dainty little glasses.

Anyway a few minutes later, Colonel Titley blew his horn and off they all clattered, the hounds squeaking, scuffing and straining and Billy bringing up the rear trying

77

to fit his size eleven pessocks into his stirrups. Of course we couldn't follow them over the fields on our bikes but we knew roughly the route they would take so we used to ride to the various points they crossed and watch them go by.

Twenty minutes after they'd set off we were sitting on the Jubilee seats at the top of Nottingham Hill waiting for them to cross the road. A few moments later the leaders emerged from the wood at the bottom of the hill. I must admit they looked quite impressive as they jumped the little hedge on to the road and disappeared into the ditch the other side. There were about twenty riders and perhaps twice as many dogs, all bunched together in a pool of golden brown. The last one across the road was Mrs Bradbury's daughter on her pony.

'Your drawers is showing,' shouted Skulker as she went by, but she stuck her nose in the air and ignored him.

We were about to get on our bikes and go to the next post, disappointed because we'd missed Billy in the main bunch of riders, when Fatty Heathershaw gave a great shout of delight.

'Look, look there he is.'

Daisy was only ambling along towards the little hedge but Billy had his huge, white behind stuck high in the air as if he was Lester Piggott riding flat out. Daisy reached the hedge and stopped. Billy peered out from behind her head, still with his behind stuck up like Ben Nevis. Then he slowly climbed off and walked towards the gate, about five yards from where Daisy had stopped.

We now realized why he'd kept his behind stuck in the air; he was obviously in agony and couldn't bear to put it on the saddle. He shuffled to the gate, his legs wide enough apart for a sheep to have run through. He climbed painfully on board Daisy again before we'd sufficiently recovered from laughing to shout at him.

'Go it Bill.'

'Do you want a cushion?'

'Rub it with a dock-leaf.'

'Have a go at side-saddle.'

He ignored us completely, his face set in concentration, either from pain or determination, I didn't know which.

They killed a fox near Caythorpe Cover. We'd left our bikes on the road and walked across. One day Old Colonel Titley had given Fatty the fox's tail, brush he called it, and we were always hoping we'd get another, though I don't know why; it wasn't much use. Well, we all sat on the grass bank near the edge of the cover and watched those horse-faced people milling around, drinking from flasks, eating triangle sandwiches and yaw-hawing about the chase. Then poor old Billy turned up. He was still on Daisy, but he'd obviously been off her a fair bit as well. He looked like an abominable mud-man, his fancy red and white gear showing only in small patches through the slimy mud; his face was like a soldier's disguised to go out on night-patrol, and he'd lost his hat. He flopped down from Daisy and sat disconsolately under a tree. I saw Colonel Titley eyeing him with a sneer of distaste on his whisky-blotched features.

'Had a tumble, Barstow?' he snapped at poor old Billy.

'Yus suh,' said Billy looking up and wiping his nose on his sleeve, leaving a worse mark than before.

'Try to keep up with the rest, there's a good fellow,' said the Colonel, but not sympathetically. Then he blew his horn and within twenty seconds the whole lot of them were belting off towards Church Hill.

'Come on, Bill, you'll be late,' I shouted.

Billy tried to struggle off his knees—he'd been careful not to let his backside touch the ground. Then he flopped down again.

'Christ, I'm knackered,' said Billy loudly and fiercely.

As soon as he'd said it we felt a bit sorry for him. He sounded more like the Co-op van Billy.

79

'Hey up, Billy,' said Fatty. 'We'll tek your hoss home and you ride on my bike.'

Billy didn't speak for a few minutes. Then he suddenly said, 'Christ, I'm buggered if I won't.'

So as dusk fell on Boxing Day we reached the village, Fatty trotting along leading Daisy, us on our bikes, and a big muddy man in hunting pink riding a battered blue boy's bike, his backside stuck in the air like a *Tour de France* winner, but only moving about five miles an hour.

Maybe at this stage Bill would have liked to forget his money and go back to being a milkman. But he couldn't; the money was a fact of his life and he had to do something with it.

So he bought a big house. It was quite a good house, at first; modern, large windows, a double garage and four bedrooms. Perhaps Bill ought to have got married or something; but he'd never had much to do with women and thought he was too old to start now. I never saw inside Bill's house but after six months the outside began to look like a garden centre. You know some houses have wagon wheels, fancy ones painted white, in the garden? Well, I'm not too keen on them myself, but I suppose one is all right. But not seventeen! You see old Bill never knew when to stop once he thought he was on to a good thing. The gnomes bred like rabbits. We tried to count them one day but it was as difficult as counting a flock of sheep. There was a big green one fishing near the gate in a little red one's earhole. The little red one was digging up the feet of another green one; perhaps he disapproved of it because it seemed to be peeing on to the multitude of goldfish in the ornamental pond. I won't describe Bill's house in detail, but it was obvious even to us old boys after six months, that he'd made a mess of it.

Anyway Bill seemed to be fairly happy with his house, despite the fact that passing strangers sometimes called to ask him the price of a wagon-wheel, a gnome or a tub of geraniums.

Having given up his hunting Bill tried other sports suitable to a wealthy man. We were never sure why he gave up golf after six months; he had lots of lessons, all the right gear and seemed quite happy at first. We knew he wasn't very good though, because if we'd nothing better to do we'd stand and watch him chipping the little white balls over his ornamental pond. He murdered a few fish and many gnomes and we used to shout, 'Good shot, Bill,' every time he hit a gnome. He used to pretend he was aiming for the gnomes if we were watching but he didn't fool us.

I don't think it was incompetence that made him give up, though; I think there might have been something in the rumour that he'd been banned for foul language, because if we hid behind the cedar tree so that he didn't know we were watching him practise, we usually picked up a few new swear words to try out on each other.

In the middle of the summer after he first won the pools Billy joined the village cricket team. He was soon a regular member of the side; well, he'd a big car which could take half the team to away matches, three brand new bats and was the only one in a complete set of whites. So he had to be in the team, didn't he?

You don't see many people carried off cricket fields, do you? Billy was a big bloke and it took half the team to carry him off after Holton's fast bowler hit him so hard in his beer-belly that the ball took several seconds to emerge and fall on the grass. He wasn't unconscious or anything like that; unconscious people don't make noises like Billy made as he laid flat on his back with his feet sticking up in the air. But he wouldn't get up; he just lay there swearing. So in the end half the team carried him off. They plopped him down under the scoreboard. Then he did

81

a very annoying thing; annoying anyway for the people who'd sweated carrying him off.

He got up and said, 'Good job my guts is made of iron,' and walked out to carry on with his innings.

He did better at cricket than at golf and hunting. One day he made sixteen not out against the YMCA. He was a liability on the field though; one day I saw him waiting to catch a hit that had sent the ball about forty feet in the air. He crouched under it, hands cupped, eyes on the ball, dead still. Everything was right, in fact, except Billy's position. The ball hit him on the head, bounced off to Norman, the captain, who caught it.

'Well passed, Billy,' shouted Skulker.

We were too far away to hear what he said but I noticed the vicar, who always played wicket-keeper, put his big red gloves over his ears and turn away.

All the cricket matches except one were against other village teams, played on oases of bumpy grass in the middle of fields of buttercups, dandelions and cow-dung. Once a year, though, there was a match on the local town's flat pitch with a proper outfield mown in neat stripes. This was the Dickson Cup Match, first round. There would have been more than one match of course, if our village ever got through to the second round. But it never did. You see most of the other teams in the cup were from the local town and were used to playing on proper pitches. I suppose they were better than our lot anyway but we'd have probably beaten them at finding the ball in a clump of daisies or nettles, or if they'd let us have our umpire, Razzer Morton, who was good at l.b.w.'s, particularly when our team was fielding.

But they had proper umpires in white coats, who counted with pebbles instead of blades of grass and who sometimes didn't even bother to say 'Not out', just grinned when our lot appealed for l.b.w.'s that Razze would have given out like a shot.

Most of the village used to turn out, though, for the Dickson Cup. There were usually plenty of spectators from the town as well, who jeered amiably when the rustics came out to field, an odd pair of white trousers, usually painters', here and there along with the occasional sweater —the vicar had one with some cricket bats across the front which he'd stolen when he was a chaplain in the army. Tim Carter always wore his milking hat, which was white and kept falling off when he ran for the ball.

Billy shook them when he turned out for us: sweater, socks, shirt, boots, all white and gleaming new.

'Hey up, one of 'em's won the pools,' shouted a local sitting in the stand. I think it was just a lucky guess. Nobody outside the village knew about Billy's win.

Well, this Holwell team scored ninety-seven in the eighteen overs allowed, which wasn't too bad for us, especially as Tim Carter had had to go off after the first over so we were only fielding with ten men. Tim had started to run after a ball that was obviously going to the boundary. In the first few strides his milking hat had fallen; he'd tried to catch it while running, had twisted himself and fallen in a heap. He didn't get up.

'Come on, get the ball, Tim,' shouted Norman.

Tim rose slowly, holding his right knee with both hands.

'What's up?' shouted Norman, getting annoyed.

'I think my bloody cartridge has gone again,' yelled Tim, and started hobbling to the dressing-room.

This caused a lot of laughter among the spectators. I didn't know why but Fatty, who was quite clever, said that 'cartridge' was the wrong word.

Our village were seven runs for five wickets down when Billy Barstow trotted out of the pavilion. To add to his gleaming gear he was carrying a brand new Gunn and Moore bat. He'd only got one pad though; I heard afterwards that this was because the people before him had been out so quickly he'd not had time to put on more than one. It wouldn't have mattered normally, because many of our team only appeared in one pad—there were only five pads in the club before Billy joined. It mattered in Billy's case, though, because he'd put his pad on the wrong leg. You see if you bat right-handed your left leg is facing down the pitch and obviously that's the one to put the pad on. Your right leg is behind you and that can usually take care of itself.

'Left-hander,' shouted the Holwell captain as Billy neared the wicket. He obviously didn't think Billy was stupid enough to put his pad on the wrong leg, so he assumed Billy was left-handed, in which case his pad would be all right.

The fielders started to change over for a left-hander. When Billy faced up right-handed they started to change back again.

'Your pad's on the wrong leg, Bill,' shouted Norman, who was not out two at the other end.

'Christ! So it is,' said Billy.

Slowly he took off his sausage-like batting gloves. Then he undid his pad. Three minutes later he'd succeeded in buckling his pad on the correct leg. It took a lot longer for him to get his batting gloves back though; there seemed to be more sausages than fingers to fit into them. The fielders changed round once more, some of them muttering about playing for time. The spectators weren't muttering though. They were yelling their disapproval.

'Get on with it; it'll be dark in a minute.'

'Come on, Bradman, it's a cricket match, not a strip-tease.'

'We haven't paid a tanner to watch a fashion show.'

At last Billy was ready to face the bowling. The first ball proved that Billy Barstow had more to him than met the eyes. He proved the lot of them, Norman, fielders, bowler and spectators wrong. It was quite a fast ball, it broke through Billy's defences and hit him on the back leg, the one without the pad.

'How's that?' yelled the whole of the Holwell team, as Billy fell in a heap in front of his wicket. Nobody had the grace to acknowledge that Billy was right about the pad after all. The spectators were laughing and jeering.

'Not out,' said the proper umpire, tossing a pebble from one hand to the other. Now if we'd had Razzer umpiring he'd have given Billy out, and then of course he wouldn't have been hit in the guts next ball. Down went Billy like a sack of tates; up went the hands of all the fielders and most of the crowd. It was a bit like fox-hunting; a sort of bloodlust was in their voices as they appealed for l.b.w. again.

And still the stupid umpire didn't give him out.

They levered Billy to his feet after another delay of two minutes. Sensibly they propped him up a little way away from his wicket so that the next ball hit the middle stump instead of Billy Barstow.

'No ball,' shouted some spectators, disappointed at the end of the spectacle.

'How's that?' yelled the whole of the Holwell team.

The proper umpire said nothing; he obviously didn't think he needed to give Billy out when his middle stump was lying flat.

'You're out, Bill,' said Norman, kindly.

'Christ, am I?' said Bill, like a boxer coming round after being knocked out.

'Thank Christ for that,' said Bill as he limped painfully to the pavilion.

His innings had lasted nineteen minutes, longer than anyone else's that night except for Norman's. Three balls had been bowled in the nineteen minutes—probably a record of some sort.

I'm not saying poor old Bill got himself half-killed because he won the pools. I know it's not as simple as that.

But I know he wouldn't have been playing cricket if he hadn't won the pools. I mean he was forty odd and he'd never played before. He just felt that he had to take up some gentleman's sport because he was rich—and the plain fact was that Billy was rotten at sport; hunting, golf, cricket, anything. Tim Carter and several others in the cricket team weren't much good, but at least they were quick enough to dodge out of the way. They wouldn't have got clouted the times poor Bill did that season. There was another thing old Bill was bad at—being rich. Perhaps you need to practise being rich or something; or at least you have to work yourself in at it.

I sometimes wonder what would have happened if I'd been telling my Dad the truth when I was reading out those 'draws' on his treble chance. Perhaps he would have been as rotten and fed up as Billy at being rich. On second thoughts, though, he could have bought me a new bike, football, cricket bat, I could have gone to the pictures every day, I could have had a pound of sweets at a time, I . . . yes, I would be all right at being rich. I think I would, anyway.

ALSO IN

General Editors: Anne and Ian Serraillier

Chinua Achebe Things Fall Apart
Douglas Adams The Hitchhiker's Guide to the Galaxy
Vivien Alcock The Cuckoo Sister; The Monster Garden; The Trial of Anna Cotman; A Kind of Thief
Margaret Atwood The Handmaid's Tale
J G Ballard Empire of the Sun
Nina Bawden The Witch's Daughter; A Handful of Thieves; Carrie's War; The Robbers; Devil by the Sea; Kept in the Dark; The Finding; Keeping Henry; Humbug
E R Braithwaite To Sir, With Love
John Branfield The Day I Shot My Dad
F Hodgson Burnett The Secret Garden
Ray Bradbury The Golden Apples of the Sun; The Illustrated Man
Betsy Byars The Midnight Fox; Goodbye, Chicken Little; The Pinballs
Victor Canning The Runaways; Flight of the Grey Goose
Ann Coburn Welcome to the Real World
Hannah Cole Bring in the Spring
Jane Leslie Conly Racso and the Rats of NIMH
Robert Cormier We All Fall Down
Roald Dahl Danny, The Champion of the World; The Wonderful Story of Henry Sugar; George's Marvellous Medicine; The BFG; The Witches; Boy; Going Solo; Charlie and the Chocolate Factory; Matilda
Anita Desai The Village by the Sea
Charles Dickens A Christmas Carol; Great Expectations
Peter Dickinson The Gift; Annerton Pit; Healer
Berlie Doherty Granny was a Buffer Girl
Gerald Durrell My Family and Other Animals
J M Falkner Moonfleet
Anne Fine The Granny Project
Anne Frank The Diary of Anne Frank
Leon Garfield Six Apprentices
Jamila Gavin The Wheel of Surya
Adele Geras Snapshots of Paradise

Graham Greene The Third Man and The Fallen Idol; Brighton Rock

Thomas Hardy The Withered Arm and Other Wessex Tales

Rosemary Harris Zed

L P Hartley The Go-Between

Ernest Hemingway The Old Man and the Sea; A Farewell to Arms

Nat Hentoff Does this School have Capital Punishment?

Nigel Hinton Getting Free; Buddy; Buddy's Song

Minfong Ho Rice Without Rain

Anne Holm I Am David

Janni Howker Badger on the Barge; Isaac Campion

Linda Hoy Your Friend Rebecca

Barbara Ireson (Editor) In a Class of Their Own

Jennifer Johnston Shadows on Our Skin

Toeckey Jones Go Well, Stay Well

James Joyce A Portrait of the Artist as a Young Man

Geraldine Kaye Comfort Herself; A Breath of Fresh Air

Clive King Me and My Million

Dick King-Smith The Sheep-Pig

Daniel Keyes Flowers for Algernon

Elizabeth Laird Red Sky in the Morning; Kiss the Dust

D H Lawrence The Fox and The Virgin and the Gypsy; Selected Tales

Harper Lee To Kill a Mockingbird

Julius Lester Basketball Game

Ursula Le Guin A Wizard of Earthsea

C Day Lewis The Otterbury Incident

David Line Run for Your Life; Screaming High

Joan Lingard Across the Barricades; Into Exile; The Clearance; The File on Fraulein Berg

Penelope Lively The Ghost of Thomas Kempe

Jack London The Call of the Wild; White Fang

Bernard Mac Laverty Cal; The Best of Bernard Mac Laverty

Margaret Mahy The Haunting; The Catalogue of The Universe

Jan Mark Do You Read Me? Eight Short Stories

James Vance Marshall Walkabout

Somerset Maugham The Kite and Other Stories

Michael Morpurgo Waiting for Anya; My Friend Walter; The War of Jenkins' Ear

How many have you read?